To Martha Kelly,
with very best wishes.

Gary Barker
12-13-83

FIRE
ON THE
MOUNTAIN

A collection of
short stories

by

GARRY BARKER

KENTUCKE IMPRINTS • BEREA, KENTUCKY • 40403

KENTUCKE IMPRINTS
Berea, Kentucky   40403

COPYRIGHT © 1983 BY GARRY BARKER

LIBRARY OF CONGRESS CATALOG CARD NUMBER
82-082038

ISBN 0-935680-12-8

DEDICATION

To "Miss Belle," Eliza Belle Cook, the teacher who loved a bashful, backward mountain boy enough to open his eyes to the joys of art and literature. She believed in me, and I still love her.

FOREWORD

Appalachia is neither a quaint, romantic land nor home-place to a people drenched in filth and ignorance. WW II, television, and new highways have forever ended the isolation; consolidated schools, social service programs, and massive federal aid have blunted most of the abject poverty and lack of education.

The old settlement schools have been replaced by modern high schools and community colleges, and the mobile home has created instant, modern housing. Poverty—and the lack of economic opportunity—handcuff the region. Coal mines and small farms are still the mainstays, and neither is enough.

In four short decades we've lived through a century of change, leapt from the 18th to the 20th Century almost over-night, moved from mule drawn sleds to jet planes and computers. We're still adjusting, trying to decide, wondering if all the changes are good, wondering what comes next.

The progress has cost our culture much of its independence, its unique coloring, its fierce pride. We are rooted to the hills in a way few outsiders can ever comprehend, and today a reverse migration is swelling our population, as those who once left come home.

The traditional mountaineer exists only in fiction. The inbred, imbecilic hillbilly is a media creature, a fundraising device for some Appalachian agencies and an easy stereotype for TV producers.

My writing makes no moral judgements. I tell stories, record memories, try to adapt the Appalachian stoicism and humor to fiction. I hope you enjoy my efforts.

Garry Barker

CONTENTS

FIRE ON THE MOUNTAIN

He caressed the fiddle, turning it gently in his calloused hands to inspect every detail. The back and sides were Birdseye Maple, painstakingly formed and sanded to glossy smoothness, and the top, with its ornate sound holes, was Spruce, geometrically striped, carefully cut and fitted. The slim neck was sturdy Maple, gracefully tapered, and the tuning pegs were Black Walnut.

"It play good?" he asked.

"Try it," grinned Willie. "Here's you a bow."

"Druther use my own, you don't mind."

"Hell, I don't care, Asy. You play 'er any way you want to."

Asa Horner, six feet eight and deceptively graceful, cradled the new fiddle under his chin and touched his bow to the strings.

The sound was sweet and sharp, full throated, and the cabin rang with the joyous sounds. He played snatches of "Sourwood Mountain" and "Cotton Eyed Joe," swung into "Red Wing," and switched to "Shove That Pig's Foot A Little Closer To The Fire," and slowed to finish with the haunting "Amazing Grace."

"Kin ye do 'Little Log Cabin In The Lane'?" begged Willie. "Hit's my favorite of all."

Asa played the request, threw in "Cluck Old Hen", and broke into two minutes of "The Devil Went Down To Georgia".

"Mighty fine, Asy," said Willie. "You shore do play good."

"Damn good fiddle," grunted Asa. "How much?"

"Bein hit's you, Asy, I reckon three hundred 'd do it."

Willie watched closely for Asa's reaction. "Worth twict that, ye know."

"I know," grinned Asa, his yellowed buck teeth protruding, "next Summer, when the tourists are here, it'll bring you five hundred."

Willie frowned and shifted the blanks he was shaping for the next fiddle. "Two hundred seventy five?"

"Two fifty," said Asa. "Cash money."

"Youre a robbin me, Asy," moaned Willie.

"You could keep it," said Asa. "Next Summer, you could —."

"Take it, damnit. Two hundred fifty and a quart of that shine you git."

"Sold," said Asa. "I'll be back up after supper."

"You'll be bringin the shine?"

"One quart, one hundred and eighty proof, clear as spring water."

"Where you git that stuff, Asy?"

"I ain't tellin," said Asa. "Feller could git shot, tellin where his shine come from."

"Ain't it the truth." Willie bit off a fresh chew. "I mind the time me and Ezry went over to—."

"I gotta be goin, Willie," interrupted Asa. "Tonight we'll talk." He smiled. "And I'll play some more, if you can spare me a toddy to get me goin."

He left quickly, and drove off humming the tune to "Fire On The Mountain." Slouched in the narrow bucket seat of the blue Jeep he resembled a graying bullfrog, heavy jowls drooping, belly squeezed in under the steering wheel, stringy gray hair hanging below the corduroy hunting cap.

Asa carried three hundred pounds on his elongated frame, and his clothes had stretched to bag loosely. The red jacket, with cartridge loops and game pockets, was soiled and wrinkled. The shapeless trousers had been green, and were worn shiny at the knees and seat. Heavy boots with thick yellow sponge soles were laced to midcalf, and he carried a Buck knife on his belt.

The Jeep was muddy and dented, showing hard use and minimal care. The back, with the jump seats folded away, was cluttered with an assortment of wrenches, pipe, rain gear, blocks of wood, a rusty skillet, an axe, and a tangle of rope. A battered case cushioned the old fiddle, and a .30—.30 Winchester carbine rode standing between the seats.

The engine growled as he downshifted to cross the creek, knobbed tires slinging mud and water as he exited, gunned up the steep cut, and dropped down to the gravel roadway.

The narrow lane followed the crest of Hogback Mountain for five miles, then dropped and curled its way down five thousand feet below to connect with the paved highway beside the railroad track. Asa was home in thirty minutes, none too soon to suit the waiting young delivery man.

Asa helped the laconic youth unload and store the shipment, paid him, and stood waiting as he methodically counted. "That's got it," he said, tucking the cash inside his fat wallet. "We got us a problem, though, Mr. Horner."

"What's wrong?" asked Asa.

"Pap don't want me deliverin no more," he said. "Too risky, crossin the line alla time. We're just gonna sell to them what comes and gits it."

"I don't reckon I got any choice," said Asa. "Tell you pap I'll be down in two weeks for my load." He watched the old Chrysler rumble away and cursed his bad luck. That evening he asked Willie how to go about hauling the moonshine.

"Where from?" asked Willie.

"South Carolina."

Willie chuckled. "How much you haulin at a time?"

"Fifty, eighty gallons, more when I can get it."

"Git ye a big old car," advised Willie. "A Mercury or Buick or Chrysler, and git one o' them Asheville mechanics to fix you up with a motor and springs and brakes. Then you bring it up here and I'll finish 'er up fer ye. You want to haul bottles er in tanks?"

"Which is better?"

"Tanks is easier to hide. Ye kin stick 'em in the floor and sich." Willie spat into the fireplace. "Bottles, they git broke too damn easy."

On his way home Asa pondered the possibility of going back to his old job, leaving the moonshine market to younger and braver men.

††††††

For twenty years Asa Horner had taught mathematics at North Carolina State University in Raleigh, pursuing his love for folklore and fiddling on weekends and during the summers. The little house on the mountain over Asheville had been a friend's summer cottage, borrowed often by Asa, purchased three years ago when the friend took a job on the West Coast. After two years of driving back and forth and winterproofing the house Asa resigned, packed his few belongings, and moved.

His savings evaporated, and in six months he was almost broke. The fiddle earned only ribbons, and Asa was ill qualified to handle most available jobs.

His supplier, a lanky farmer from Old Fort, sat Asa up as a moonshine distributor, arranging the reliable South Carolina source and referring Asheville area customers to the cottage on the mountain. The profits were sizeable and tax free. Asa paid forty dollars per gallon, delivered in bulk, and sold the shine for upwards of forty per quart. He bought the new Jeep, ran water to the cottage, and had over ten thousand dollars in the lard can under the floor.

He could not quit now.

††††††

The Cadillac was baby blue with a white roof, a 1972 Coupe DeVille with a solid body and blown engine. Asa paid two hundred, plus a thirty dollar tow bill to move the car to Banjo's in West Asheville.

The estimate was seven thousand dollars.

"What do I get for that?" gulped Asa.

The grizzled Banjo ticked off the changes. A new five hundred horsepower engine; heavy duty radiator, brakes, and transmission; a tuned racing suspension, with air shocks to level heavy loads; belted steel tires and a "thirty-thirty" warranty.

"Thirty feet er thirty seconds," grinned Banjo.

"What about a paint job?" asked Asa.

"Best to leave it be," said Banjo, "specially iffen ye ain't wantin nobody to notice ye."

Asa blushed. "Guess you're right."

It took three weeks. Asa gambled, and drove the Jeep across the state line to pick up his scheduled shipment. He sweated and his stomach churned until he was safely home and unloaded.

"It's not worth it, Asa," insisted Penelope Nye, his semi-steady lover. "Why do you put yourself through such things?"

"Money," said Asa. "To get me free time to fiddle and lay in bed with you."

"Pull out," she begged.

"Can't," he said. "Paid Banjo four thousand already."

Penelope drove him to pick up the Cadillac and followed him up the mountain to Willie's.

"Down by the river," Willie told him," we kin git tanks and hoses and stuff. "Better bring about five hunnert cash." They came with the Jeep stacked full, and Willie's work took four days.

He showed it proudly. "Four twenty-five gallon tanks, all hid in the body. Ye fill 'em over here, inside the panel. Drain plug's under the frame, there. She's all set, Asy. When's yer first run?"

"Tomorrow," choked Asa.

††††††

That night his fiddle was mournful, and not even Penelope's wet kisses could dispel his fears.

Asa was up at dawn, checking and rechecking the Cadillac, topping off the gas tank, gauging the tires, cleaning the windshield. At noon he could wait no longer. He strapped the leather pouch with the four thousand dollars safely to his left leg and drove South.

The car was responsive and agile, flatly slipping around the tight curves, accelerating with a rush, stopping at the touch of the brake. He suddenly realized he was speeding, slowed to the limit, and crossed through Greeneville at one.

Loaded and on the road home by three, Asa stopped to pump up the air shocks and eliminate the sag. Even with its one hundred gallons aboard the car was easy to drive, and he hummed fiddle tunes as he climbed the mountain toward Flat Rock. The roadblock was a total surprise; he braked, swallowed, and tried to stay cool.

The trio of gray uniformed troopers looked larger than life, standing casually by the roadside, checking each vehicle closely. Asa had his liscense ready.

"You the fiddle player?"

Asa glanced up in surprise. "I play."

"I saw you last summer at the folk festival," said the trooper, "and I like the old stuff you played."

"Why, thank you," said Asa. "Come by sometime and I'll show you my collection of old tunes."

"I'll do that, Mr. Horner." He waved Asa through. "Have a good trip."

Asa's underwear was soaked through, stuck to his bottom and dampening his pants. He drove cautiously, and was home in less than an hour. At Willie's he drained the shine into the new storage tank buried behind the cabin.

They sipped a sample. "Damn," said Willie. "This is better'n what you been gittin.''

For two months, until Spring began to break, the new deal worked perfectly, with Willie taking ten percent for his work. "Shore pays better'n fiddle makin,'' he observed. "Asy, we could handle twice as much, now we got the car all fixed and the tank in place.''

"Forget it!'' Asa was firm. "We can't risk any more, Willie.''

"Hell, I kin drive,'' grunted Willie to himself as Asa left. "Ain't no sense in me doin without when theys easy cash to be had.''

He scratched his chin thoughtfully, and the next day drove his old Chevy to the store and used the phone to arrange a pickup. "It'll be atter dark,'' he told them, "and I'll be drivin.''

Asa and Penelope left for Asheville to hear a new young fiddler play, and the cottage was dark when Willie arrived. He took four thousand dollars from the lard can, leaving an IOU, and found the keys to the Cadillac. Twenty miles down the road he stopped and leaned on the horn ring. "Hurry it up, Bessie,'' he howled, "you and me's got a date.'' He waved the quarter empty bottle. "Brung a little antifreeze.'' He drank again as she ran to the car.

Bessie Cole had serviced Willie's needs for twenty-five years, and loved nothing better than a night ride and some sipping whiskey, and Willie provided both. The bottle was empty before Flat Rock, and another from under the floormat kept them happy. Willie drove with grand, sweeping movements, tires screaming. Bessie snuggled close.

After the tanks were filled Willie felt even better. The Cadillac was humming, Bessie was warm and willing; and the April freshness blew in through the open windows.

At the base of the state line mountain he saw the flashing blue lights behind him.

"Hang on, Bessie!'' he yelled. "Revenooers!'' The engine roared as he punched the accelerator, and the Cadillac surged away from the surprised South Carolina highway patrolman. He grinned and accelerated, figuring to quickly overtake the old car and make the arrest. As his speedometer passed 115 he peered after the vanishing taillights. "Damn," he muttered. "That thing must be doing 130 or more." He radioed the North Carolina patrol. "White on blue Cadillac, North Carolina tags, headed your way at about 140. No known warrants. I just wanted to tell him his brake light was dead and he took off like a bat outa hell. He's all yours, fellers." He turned at the line and drove back south, smiling.

Willie slid up the ramp to I-26 with his foot on the floor, almost rearending the waiting cruiser before he swung to the left, passed, and drove with one hand, stroking Bessie with the other, singing at the tops of his lungs. He left the Interstate at the Asheville Airport, took US 25 to the Blue Ridge Parkway, and a pair of Park Service Rangers joined the chase. Radios crackled as the frustrated law officers tried to coordinate their pursuit.

Willie lost a headlight as he broke the roadblock at US 70, shunting a cruiser off into the weeds and sending two troopers diving for cover, and ripped off a muffler as he bounced and skidded across the cement barriers. After three miles he braked hard, swerved right, and followed the narrow road by the railroad tracks. He switched off the lights.

"Lord!" screamed Bessie. "You're gonna kill us both!"

Two tons of metal soared into the air as they topped the sudden rise. "Damn," grunted Willie. "Fergot about that hill!"

The front tires hit hard, flattened, and exploded. The Cadillac slued sideways, hubcaps flying, clipped a row of bushes from the muddy bank, and finally stopped, rear wheels dangling over the edge of the steep bluff.

Willie grabbed Bessie in a fierce hug. "What in Hell are you doin!" she screeched.

"Tell them cops," said Willie, "that we's jist out here parkin."

††††††

The patrol car followed Asa up his drive.

"Mr. Asa Horner?"

"Yes. What's wrong?"

"You own a 1972 Cadillac, blue on—?"

"It's mine. What's happened?"

The trooper relaxed into a slow grin. "Some drunk old coot used your car to outrun ever policeman from the South Carolina border to Swannanoa."

Asa blanched. "Willie Sims?"

"That's him. Don't know if we'd ever have caught him if he hadn't had a blowout."

"Is he hurt?"

"Not to speak of. Just a bump behind his ear. We had to subdue him. He's over at the jail, asking for you."

"The car?"

"Being towed. You can claim it in the morning at the highway patrol garage."

"Was Willie—why were you chasing him?"

"Started out over a busted brake light." The trooper laughed. "Now, they got a list of charges ranging from drunken driving to resisting arrest to damaging public property."

"What damage?"

"He killed a cruiser. Took that old Caddy and knocked it clean off the highway into a ditch."

Asa groaned.

He saved the crucial question for Willie, still groggy as they sat in the little visitors cubicle at the jail.

"Did you have a shipment?"

"Hunnert gallon," hissed Willie. "They ain't noticed it yit."

Asa was trembling. "You mean they've got a hundred gallons sitting out there at the station?"

Willie grinned. "They ain't a goin to know it lessen you tell 'em. These young fellers, they ain't got good noses."

Asa bailed him out, and early the next morning they were at the patrol garage to claim the Cadillac. Sagging to the front, it sat alone in the gravel lot behind the garage. The headlight dangled, and broken limbs clung to the rear bumper. A spreading puddle was underneath.

"My God," moaned Asa. He crawled under to check the leak. "Valve's broken," he muttered. "It's steady comin out, Willie."

"Mornin, fellers." Asa slammed his head into the frame as he scrambled out. "Come to git the old Caddy?"

"Yes," said Asa. "I paid the tow and storage."

"Better git it to a shop," said the foreman of the garage, "and git that hole in the transmission plugged up."

"I will," said Asa, taking the man by the arm and leading him away. "Say, can I use your telephone to call a wrecker?"

The Cadillac had been gone for thirty minutes when one of the mechanics stopped to light a cigar and tossed the burning match into the gravel.

Flames lept, blue and flickering, spreading with a sudden "swoosh" and blast of air. "Yeeoow!" screamed the mechanic. "What in Hell is this?" He danced clear of the flames, slapping at his smoking pants legs. "What kinda damn transmission fluid does that son-of-a-bitch use?"

The fire died and left a circle of scorched rock.

†††††

The Cadillac rested on concrete blocks.

Willie rigged a hose and opened the valve, draining the clear liquid into milk cans, loading them into Asa's Jeep for the trip to Hogback Mountain.

Willie tabulated gloomily. "Four cans is eighty gallon, and half another'n makes ninety. Spilt ten gallon, more or less, Asy."

"That's four hundred dollars, Willie. Plus two tires is $250, and $175 for the muffler and pipe makes $425, and fixing the fender will run $175 or so. You owe me $675 for the car." He grinned. "Ninety gallons'll bring about $11,000, and your cut would be $1,100. Pay for the car and that leaves, oh, $525. Your fine will be maybe $1,000, so you're out about $500 for the night. Was it worth it?"

"Damn near it," swore Willie. "Hit was like the old days, there fer a while."

"Get in," said Asa. "Let's get what's left of this stuff up to the tank." He drove the Jeep carefully, protecting his valuable cargo.

††††††

Four men in a dusty Bronco followed the Jeep.

"They're gonna take us right to it, George," said the driver.

Two federal agents and two sheriff's deputies huddled to peer out the window.

"That old fool thinks we didn't notice," chuckled George, the senior deputy. "Hell, everbody in two mile knowed what he was haulin. That old Cadillac musta had fifty gallon in it somewheres."

Agent Earl Smith, at the wheel, grunted. "Shoulda arrested him, too, while we had 'im with the stuff." He downshifted and began the steep climb.

"Naw," said George. "Willie's gonna show us where the rest of it is now. We'll git maybe a hunnert gallon, and put old Willie away fer five years."

"What about the other feller?"

"Horner? Hell, he wouldn't know shine if he was settin a tubfull. He's one a them rich fellers that come here to live the simple life."

"You sure he's not the man in charge?"

"Hell, he don't need the money," said George. "All he wants to do is play that fiddle. Willie's our man."

††††††

Asa backed the Jeep close to the rhododendren thicket, and together they emptied the cans down the concealed inlet.

Willie cackled. "Ain't nobody'd believe we got a 500 gallon tank down under there." He closed the spout and pulled the limbs back over to cover it. "Yessir, me and you, we done it right, Asy. Got it right on tap, right under their damn feet, and can't none of them see a thing."

Asa pulled the Jeep down to the cabin. "I could use a drink," he said.

Willie rinsed two peanut butter jars, and opened the door under the kitchen sink. He stooped, twisted the faucet concealed under a towel, and filled both glasses, and lifted one up to the light to inspect it.

"Clear as water," he said. "Asy, this was some fine idea, runnin the line into the kitchen here. Hell, nobody'd ever believe it."

They drank, gulping the raw whiskey.

"Bring out a fiddle," said Asa, "and we'll damn well celebrate."

He refilled the glasses, and closed the door.

††††††

The three mudsplattered men crawled back into the Bronco.

"Goddamnit, Smitty, next time I'm doin the drivin," growled George.

"How am I supposed to know," protested Smith, "that they ain't but one place to cross? That creek don't *look* deep."

"Shut up and drive," grunted George. "We've done give 'em time to hide the stuff."

††††††

Willie raised his hand, shushing Asa.

"Sombody comin," he said. He quickly rinsed the glasses and stepped out to the porch to watch the muddy Bronco park beside the Jeep. "It's the law," he whispered. "Keep a fiddlin, Asy."

"Mornin, fellers," sang out Willie. "What brings youens up to Hogback?"

Asa scraped busily, playing "Fire On The Mountain" extra fast.

"You know why we're here, Willie," said George. "Save us all a lot of trouble iffen ye'd jist show us where ye keep the shine."

"Shine?" Willie shook his head sadly. "Law, George, I ain't had no good sippin whiskey in fifteen year."

Asa played "What A Friend We Have In Jesus." dragging the bow mournfully across the strings.

"Willie, we know ye was haulin, last night. What's in them milk cans yonder?"

"Nothin," grinned Willie. "Them's some Asy got fer me. I paint 'em up and sell 'em to the tourists. Good money. Why, I recall—."

"Shut up, Willie," grunted George. "And tell that fool to quit playin that fiddle."

"Fool? George, that yonder's Asy Horner, what teached at the University fer twenty year. He's a wonderous smart man, George."

Asa put down the fiddle and walked outside.

"Howdy, men. Somethin I can do for ye?"

"You the one owns that Cadillac?"

"It's mine."

"You're under arrest."

"What for?"

"Runnin moonshine."

Asa chuckled. "That old Caddy is down to the house on

blocks. And, gentlemen, you won't find any moonshine anywhere in it."

"That's the damn truth," muttered George. "We watched
'em empty it all out."

"Search this area," ordered Smith. "The stuff has to be
here."

"Hep yesef," grunted Willie. "But ye ain't gonna find nothin."

The search lasted two hours, and was fruitless.

"Tol ye," grinned Willie. "You fellers want some coffee?"

††††††

Penelope and Bessie came for the celebration, and the liquor
flowed free and quick. Willie built a fire to ward off the night
chill, and Asa played with a new intensity.

He used up his repertoire by midnight, and started over.

Asa fiddled fast, slow, loud, soft, sad, and happy. Greased
by liberal doses of 180 proof, his hands fairly flew, and the
sweetest of sounds flowed out across the Mountain. He played
"Old Dan Tucker", "Sally Ann", "Fox On The Run", and a
wailing assortment of Bob Wills tunes, sweating profusely and
tapping his foot 'till his toes ached. He fiddled "White Light-
nin", "Sugar In The Gourd", "Sallie Goodin", and "Turkey
In The Straw". and "Bucking Mule".

Willie danced, pranced, kicked and wheeled around the
cabin, swinging Bessie and yelling encouragement.

††††††

"Listen at 'em," said George. "Them in there all warm and
raisin hell, and us layin out here freezin."

"Don't go blamin me," grunted Smith. "I wanted to get 'em
while they was loadin up. *You* the one wanted to foller 'em up
here. Lead us right to it, you said."

"Damnit, iffen you could drive, and hadn't a got stuck, I'd a caught 'em red handed."

"Hell," scoffed Smith. "What's that tune, George?"

"Red Wing," said George. "He sure plays that thing good."

"At least we're gettin a free concert," said Smith. "We ain't gonna get nothin else."

By three Asa was slowed, dragging the bow softly, blinking at the firelight, barely able to lift his head.

"Do 'Little Log Cabin'," said Willie.

"Bring me another drink first," said Asa. "I'm powerful thirsty."

Willie stumbled to the kitchen.

"Look at that, would you?" Smith whistled. "A damn faucet, right in the house. No wonder we never found it. They got a straight line to wherever it's hid."

Willie filled Asa's glass, but did not get the faucet closed.

The moonshine ran steadily, spilling out across the floor, trickling through the doors and spreading.

"You're all under arrest!" Smith held the .38 in his hand, glaring as he shoved open the cabin door.

"Son of a bitch," groaned Willie. "Hit's that revenooer again."

"We got ye this time, Willie," smiled George. "We seen ye a drawin shine outa that tap in the kitchen."

Asa fumbled for a match to light the cigarette.

"Here," grinned George. He flipped a box of wooden matches to Asa. "You might as well smoke 'fore we takes ye in."

Asa sucked the cigarette to life, and tossed the match to the floor.

The fire exploded.

The moonshine had run through the kitchen into the living room, a quarter inch deep in the floor, and the flames leaped to the ceiling.

"Run!" screamed Penelope.

Asa looked to Willie. "The tank!"

They jumped to the door, followed closely by George and Smitty, and dived for the bushes, dragging the women.

Asa still clutched the fiddle as he rolled.

†††††

The 500 gallon tank, three fourths full, lifted a half acre of mountain as it ignited.

George stared, his mouth open.

As far away as Asheville and Old Fort, there were reports.

"Ball o' fire," said one caller to the highway patrol. "Hit lit up nigh alla Hogback, I swear."

A Delta captain called the Asheville Airport to ask about the orange glow, swinging his 727 south to miss the turbulance.

From Montreat, Blue Ridge, and even Lake Junaluska, frightened callers warned of the end of the world.

Billy Graham, thankfully, was not at home.

†††††

The fiddle sang sadly, piercing the night with its wail, drawing out the deepest emotions from the five listeners. The ashes of Willie's cabin glowed, snapping on occasion, letting the fire die gradually.

George and Smitty lay on the charred slope, grateful to be alive, wondering who'd have to pay for the smoking Bronco.

Bessie was curled in Willie's arms, still sobbing, and Penelope sat close to Asa, ducking the bow as he fiddled.

The moon was full, and across the ridges of the Smokies, dogs howled in sympathy.

Asa stopped abruptly.

"Why ain't you fellers gone?" he asked of Smitty. "We'd rather be alone, if you don't mind."

They left quietly, walking toward lower ground.

Willie groaned through the darkness.

"Hit's all gone, Asy. My house, my car, everything."

"We still got the Cadillac, Partner," said Asa. "We can start over."

"Somehow that don't hep a lot right now," said Willie. "You still got the fiddle?"

"Right here," said Asa.

"Would ye play 'Amazing Grace'?"

The fiddle recalled the bagpipes of the highland settlers, and Willie wept softly.

They sat in total silence.

††††††

It was midsummer, the peak of the tourist season, and Willie stood kneedeep in sawdust, humming as he shaped the pattern for another fiddle. Asa's back porch was a good workshop, close enough to the city to allow the tourists to visit, and sales were booming.

The Cadillac, still on blocks, was weedchoked and rusty, a picturesque prop to entertain the buyers.

Asa nudged the wheelbarrow closer, shoveled it full of sawdust, rolled it to the bin near the cellar door, and dumped. He returned, stood on the porch, and wiped the sweat from his brow with a sopping handkerchief. "Seen 'em yet today, Willie?"

"Two. Up on the hill yonder, same place as always."

"They ain't givin up, are they?"

Willie chuckled. "Makes it a little more fun, workin right under their noses like this."

"Sawdust burner works mighty good," said Asa.

"Yep," said Willie. "Hit's a fine way to keep the place clean."

Asa took another load to the bin, and slipped inside the cellar.

The sawdust fired burner, built with the expert assistance of technicians from North Carolina State University, would be the furnace come winter. A series of traps and afterburners eliminated all smoke, and a fan sucked away any odors and vented into the sewer line. The coil was disguised as water lines; the new still was totally modern and ecologically sound, a tribute to contemporary technology and Willie's master knowledge of stilling.

On a small shelf sat rows of boxes. "Blue Diamond Fiddle Strings." Each box contained a full set of strings, as promised, and a tin pint container labeled "Fiddle Wax." Most of the wax was 180 proof.

Asa tasted the clear drops collecting in the vat, and rejoined Willie. "Good run," he grunted.

A dusty car rolled up the drive, and two middle-aged farmers climbed out, one carrying a battered fiddle case.

"Howdy, Jacob," said Willie. "Good to see ye again, Enos."

"How do," said Jacob. "I'm a needin strangs fer this here fiddle, Willie. And some more wax."

"How many sets you needin, Jacob."

"Bout four, I 'spect."

Willie bagged the four cartons in a sack printed "Sims & Horner Music Supplies" and sat it on the railing. "That'll be fifty dollar, Jacob," he said. "Strangs, they went up some."

"Hit's worth it to get gooduns," grinned Jacob. He counted five wrinkled tens from a leather pouch. "You tune 'er fer me, Asy?"

"Sure thing, Jacob."

Asa held the worn instrument gently, plucking and adjusting, then reached for the bow.

The young agent groaned. "Is that the only song he knows?"

His partner grinned. "Hell, at least we get free entertainment while we're settin out here."

"We gonna stop that car?"

"What for? Hell, it'll just be more fiddle strings. I'm gettin tired of all these musicians cussin me out. Willie ain't sellin no shine down there noway. Only reason we're here is Smitty still ain't got over that night up on Hogback."

†††††††

Asa's foot was tapping and the bow danced across the strings. Willie grinned his approval, and Jacob and Enos nodded rhythm.

In squeaky, leaping cadence, the music sang out across the trees.

†††††††

"What in Hell's the name of that tune?" grumbled the agent.
George chuckled. "Fire On The Mountain."

THE WINNER

"Two thousand dollars, as she sets."

The garage was dim and cluttered, and dust caked the frame of the battered yellow motorcycle. Elroy chewed his lower lip, sighed, mentally balanced his checkbook, and reviewed his debts.

"Parts too?" he asked.

"Everthing. Nobody wants one o' these things no more. They was the best, onct, but now. . .she's yourn if ye want her."

"I'll take it," said Elroy. "I'll give you a check for five hundred now and bring the rest on Saturday." He pulled his checkbook, wrote quickly, and handed the paper to Orville Creech.

The little grease-stained man studied the check and grinned. "The Reverend Elroy Wheelright? I never knowed that, Elroy."

"Most people don't, Orville." Elroy smiled. "I'm not planning to race it. I'll make it into a street bike." He laughed. "A fast one, by golly, but street legal."

Orville wiped dust from the humped tank, and squinted as he inspected the heavy tube frame. He shook his head, spat, and chuckled. "Better git ye some ear plugs, Elroy. This old smoker sounds like fifty chain saws runnin all at once."

Elroy smiled happily. "Ain't that the truth?"

†††††

The restoration of the Yamaha engrossed Elroy Wheelright

for four months. He stripped the bike down to the frame, checked every weld, and carefully rebuilt the low slung 250 cc road racer. New forks, shocks, chain, expansion chambers, and gas tank strained his budget, and the potent engine was delivered to Eddie Walker for rebuilding.

"Danged smoker," grumbled Eddie. "Why didn't you buy a real bike, Elroy?"

"I always wanted one of these," said Elroy. "I saw them run, once, down at Daytona, and every since then I've been looking."

The late '60's Yamaha was updated for safety. Disc brakes were added to both ends, and cast aluminum wheels replaced the bent spokes. Sticky Pirelli road tires, a six speed transmission, and lights were added. The paint was flat black and glossy orange, and all chrome was replated.

Late on a Saturday, in May, the job was done. Elroy finished fine tuning the cold engine, went back inside to strap on his old Bell helmet and snug gloves, took a deep breath, and rolled the Yamaha down the steep drive.

Halfway down he released the clutch and the engine came to life, rasping and blowing thick streams of blue smoke. At the foot of the drive Elroy waited, warming the oil, grinning as he blipped the throttle. The lights flicked on, a worn boot notched the shifter down, the tach climbed easily to 3,000, and Elroy released the clutch. The bike jerked forward, eager and responsive, but Elroy restrained himself. He rode slowly, east on US 70, through Oteen and under the Blue Ridge Parkway, his heart pounding as he sensed the power of the Yamaha. East of the city Elroy dropped quickly down the entrance ramp to Interstate 40 and opened the throttle.

With a snarling bellow the bike surged forward. At eighty Elroy shifted to fourth, at 100 mph he scooted through the traffic and found the open, moonlit highway. Bent forward, smiling, Elroy hugged the Yamaha as the speedometer crept past 130 and kept climbing.

The North Carolina Highway Patrol trooper blinked and reached for his mike. "Damned if I know just what it was," he gasped, "but something just passed me at 130. Motorcycle, of some sort, headed west on I-40."

At the West Asheville Interchange two cruisers were waiting. Elroy saw the blinking blue lights, slowed, geared down, cut across the median and spun back out onto pavement, skidding as he accelerated hard, yelling happily as the Yamaha roared through the gears. The pursuit car was in the other lane. Elroy grinned, listened to the sirens, gunned the Yamaha and swung onto the Charlotte Highway Exit. The tires screeched their protest as Elroy wheeled up to the Blue Ridge Parkway and turned left. He drove rapidly, leaning into the tight curves at over 100 mph, smiling at the precise handling of the bike. After two miles he checked his mirrors, slowed, shut off the light and found the logging trail. The engine shrieked as he slipped the clutch to climb the ditch embankment, then clattered as Elroy drove into the pine grove.

From his quiet overlook Elroy watched the futile chase of the highway patrol. When the flurry of blue lights ended, he sighed, strapped his helmet back on, and rode slowly down the back road past the zoo. He slipped across the highway, and followed the golf course fairway until he came to his steep driveway. Elroy scooted up the hill, headlight off, and parked in his dark garage. The hot engine clicked as it cooled. Elroy shrugged off the helmet and lit a cigarette, sucked the smoke deep in his lungs, and relaxed, grinning.

"Oh, my, Brother Wheelright." Elroy spun, and smiled as he saw Aggie Patton watching him. "Smoking again, I see," she said waspishly. "That's a nasty habit, Elroy." She walked closer. "Well? How does it run?"

Elroy found his voice. "Like a scalded dog, Miss Aggie."

"Good." Aggie bent low to inspect the Yamaha. "Maybe now you'll find time to visit your neighbors again." She stood erect, all five feet, bolt upright. "And just when do I get my ride?"

"Soon, Miss Aggie. Real soon. I have to get a license plate and insurance first."

"You do that," ordered Aggie. "Now, young man, don't you have a sermon to prepare?"

"Yes, ma'am, Miss Aggie," chuckled Elroy. "And, for a change, I'm in a mood to do it."

"Law, Elroy," sighed Aggie. "Sometimes I wonder if you're in the right business."

†††††

Marcus Ellington, pastor of the Hillcrest United Church, also wondered about his assistant. Sunday morning he watched and frowned as Elroy tried to quietly ease his blue Plymouth into the church parking lot, dual exhausts throbbing, engine shaking as the slow idle bogged down the cam.

"Will he ever grow up?" groaned Ellington. He shook his shaggy head. "I think not."

The hiring of Elroy Wheelright had been Ellington's effort to better relate to the younger members of his congregation, to assure them that he—firm and fifty, mellow and conservative—was also hip and up-to-date. Elroy had come from a campus ministry at a small college fifty miles north, a school which had invited the lanky young minister to leave—as soon as possible—just after the president had discovered that the college's auto shop had been serving as Elroy's speed center, and that a pit crew of ministerial students had been helping with the black Camaro racer.

The college had been Elroy's second assignment. His first, a small church near Spruce Pine, had been shocked to find their minister at the staging line of the Smoky Park Raceway, crouched over the wheel of a fat tired Dodge known for miles as the "hot shoe preacher," a lead footed drag racer.

Elroy Wheelright was a native of the North Carolina mountains, a lifelong fan of Junior Johnson and Banjo Matthews,

Fireball Roberts and Maurice Petty, the front wave of stock car racing. Elroy haunted the little dirt tracks, raced a '53 Ford when he was thirteen, and in college had convinced the school to sponsor his quarter miler as an experiment in innovative evangalism.

Strong feelings drew Elroy to the ministry, a deep love for people and concern over the injustice he saw around him. He had worked well in the rural areas, but had been uneasy about taking the job in Asheville and mingling with the old, established money of the aristocratic city.

After two years Elroy was still undecided, grateful for the huge salary but worried about the honesty of his service to the upper middle class audience. Elroy was suspect in many areas. He was a bachelor, living alone in the hillside chalet, somewhat unkempt and ill at ease in formal clothes, a soft voiced speaker who could not arouse the emotions of his congregation.

Ellington scowled as he saw Elroy's stained fingers. "Good morning, son," he said tiredly. "When are you going to sell that hot rod and get yourself somethin a mite more respectable?"

"I got my eye on this little Datsun," grinned Elroy. "A 240-Z with racing suspension, and —."

"I was thinkin more of a Buick," said Ellington.

"Could be," mused Elroy. "In '66 they built a 425 Wildcat that would—."

"Go to work, Elroy," sighed Ellington. He stopped, and frowned. "Be in my office at nine Monday morning."

Elroy spent Sunday afternoon cleaning and adjusting the Yamaha, listless and deep in thought, trying to work up a strong presentation for the evening meeting of the men of the church. At seven he drove to the chapel, nervously greeted his parishioners, and took the podium.

After a hesitant start, Elroy soared. He spoke passionately of becoming one with God, of the deep thrill of total release to a greater spirit, of the ultimate personal joy of absolute release. When he finished, there was a hush in the room, then a surge of hearty congratulations.

Elroy smiled, then went home to sit at the table until dawn. He drove restlessly through the mountains until eight, then showered and met the pastor at nine.

"Elroy, my boy, git on in here!" Ellington was glowing, beaming with pride and delight. "Russ Cox called me last night! You wowed 'em, son! Way to go!"

Elroy twisted away from the pumping handshake. "Please, sir," he mumbled. "I have to tell you something. Last night, when I was talking, and got everybody so excited, I. . .I wasn't talking about God. I just told them how it feels to ride a fast motorcycle."

Ellington stared, then burst out laughing. "Elroy," he finally gasped, "You have, at long last, figured it out. Let me tell you something." He leaned closer, and almost whispered. "Yesterday mornin, when I was doin my best preachin, do you know what I was thinkin about?"

"No," said Elroy. "What?"

"I was lookin right at that plump little Jane Westcott, imaginin what it'd be like if I was . . . aw, you know."

"You were? I mean . . . you did?"

"I was *thinkin*, Elroy. That's how I always get myself fired up. I find some good lookin woman out there, and . . ."

"I get the idea," grunted Elroy. "Doesn't that bother you? Being dishonest?"

"Why, no. Should it?"

"Look here, Elroy," said Ellington. "A preacher, he's got to be good at preachin. Ain't no way I could do it, ever Sunday, without a little inspiration." He winked. "My way's lots safer, Elroy. That motorcycle, it could kill a man."

"Sir, I'm seriously considering leaving the ministry." Elroy stood, stiff and angry. "I'm not worthy."

"Think about it first," advised Ellington. "Good money, good hours . . . don't go off half cocked, Elroy, specially now that you're gettin the hang of preachin."

†††††

For two more weeks, Elroy pondered. To relieve the tension he drove the sleek Yamaha, slashing through the darkness at full throttle, giving the state highway patrol fits of anxiety and frustration. Aggie persisted, wanted her promised ride on the bike, but Elroy hesitated to drive during the daylight hours.

"Why?" asked Aggie.

Elroy grinned sheepishly. "They might be looking for a certain orange Yamaha. They *are* looking, Aggie."

Finally he relented, at dusk on Saturday. Aggie fussed over stiff denims and worn boots, and Elroy adjusted a helmet down to fit over her tight curls. "Just hang loose, Aggie," he advised. "Sway with the bike. You'll get the hang of it in a little while."

"Don't you go worrying about me, Elroy," sniffed Aggie. "In 1937 I owned an Indian, and rode it all over these hills."

"You did?"

Aggie blushed and giggled. "I also had a Harley, in the forties. But I never rode one of these foreign jobs. Looks awful puny."

"It's not like your old Harley," laughed Elroy. "But, Aggie, this little orange monster is the fastest thing you'll ever sit on."

"Show me," said Aggie. "It's dark now."

Elroy could barely tell he was carrying a passenger, and he quickly threaded through the traffic. "It's awful noisy," yelled Aggie. "And it shakes."

"Just you wait," laughed Elroy.

Leaving the last stoplight he accelerated hard, squatting the wailing Yamaha, and he hit the Interstate ramp at eighty. "Faster!" laughed Aggie. "Open it up, Elroy!"

Elroy hit sixth gear at 100 mph, cruising easily, and Aggie hugged close as he swept through the tightly banked curves. In twenty minutes they were well west of Asheville, approaching a particularly winding ten mile stretch. Elroy eased off the throttle.

"What's wrong?" yelled Aggie. "Scared?"

Elroy laughed, downshifted, and the Yamaha leapt out from the curve. Elroy braked quickly, swung left to pass the slower car, and groaned as the blue lights flicked on behind him. "Cops, Aggie," he grunted. The bike slowed.

"No!" shrieked Aggie. "Don't stop, Elroy!"

The blue lights were closing in. "Please, Elroy," gasped Aggie. "Outrun 'em!"

"Hang on," said Elroy.

The surprised trooper watched twin puffs of exhaust smoke pour out, heard a snarl, and blinked as the Yamaha shot away in the darkness. He grabbed his mike. "It's him again," he yelled. "Got a passenger, too. Maybe tonight we'll get him."

Four more troopers rolled to join the chase.

Elroy was floating, timeless and removed, driving better than ever before. The nimble Yamaha responded to every touch, every sway, cornered with flat precision and accelerated with a rush. Aggie clung to him trembling with excitement.

They easily outdistanced the first cruiser, but two more were waiting at Waynesville. Elroy swerved, crossed the median, circled the waiting cars and headed back toward Asheville at 120. They lost the pursuit in the curves, but could not find an escape route. Back in heavy traffic Elroy slowed. "It's about over, Aggie," he said softly. "Want to surrender before we get somebody hurt?"

She nodded, and Elroy eased the Yamaha off the roadway, stopped under a security light, and heeled the bike over on its kickstand. He lifted Aggie off, and they sat together on the guard rail, smiling and waiting. The first cruiser roared to a stop and the trooper rolled out, crouching, service revolver drawn.

"Hands on your heads!" he barked. "Don't make a move."

"Yes, officer," Aggie said primly. "I guess you'll want to

search me, too?"

††††††

Six striped state patrol Fords, lights blinking, encircled the motorcycle and the small crowd gathered under the light. Elroy and Aggie were handcuffed, quiet in the back seat of a cruiser, and a van was loading the Yamaha. A burly trooper, grinning, opened the door. "Miss Aggie Patton? *The* Miss Aggie? You were my third grade teacher."

"Why, yes," said Aggie. "You're Billy Weaver."

"That's right." He blushed. "Come on outa there, Miss Aggie." Gently he unlocked the cuffs and unsnapped the heavy helmet. "What in the world were you doin?" he asked.

"Aren't you going to unlock Reverend Wheelright?" asked Aggie.

"*Reverend* Wheelright? Him?"

"Brother Elroy Wheelright," snapped Aggie. "Assistant pastor of the Hillcrest Church."

"Oh, no," groaned Weaver. "A preacher and a 76 year old schoolteacher."

"What?" growled the captain.

"You heard me." Weaver grinned. "Captain, this is Miss Aggie. She was a teacher of mine. *She* says the night rider here is a minister."

"I am," Elroy said quietly.

"Good Lord," snapped the captain. "Get 'em outa here before some nosy reporter hears about this."

"Where do I take 'em?"

"Lock him up. Take Miss Patton home."

"Oh, no, you don't," said Aggie. "I go wherever Elroy goes."

The blushing captain took a deep breath, and shrugged. "Lock 'em both up."

Aggie beamed. "Elroy," she chirped, "we're going to the big

house."

Elroy used his phone call to tell Marcus Ellington, and to resign. Ellington accepted.

Aggie called her sister, then insisted she be booked, finger-printed, and locked in a cell. Lela Patton arrived with a TV crew in tow, and the story was aired at eleven.

The trial was quick and well publicized. All charges against Aggie were dropped; Elroy was fined $2,000 and his license was taken for two years..

The flurry of favorable publicity puzzled Elroy. Marcus Wellington made a personal visit, scowling at the clutter of the house, to offer reinstatement. "It'd be perfect, Elroy. A preach-er is human. You'd be a Hell's Angel in the pulpit. Son, we'd have a full house ever Sunday." Four other churches discreetly called. Elroy, mildly shocked, declined the offers.

Confused, distracted, Elroy groaned under the burden of his infamy and his financial woes. "It's not just the fine," he told Aggie. "There's the lawyer, court costs, and the loan payments. Rent, food. . ." He shrugged. "I'll have to sell the bike, for one thing. I can't stay in the ministry. I've got to leave and make a new start."

Aggie pondered. "How much?"

"To get started?"

"For the Yamaha."

"Oh, six or seven thousand. I still owe two."

"What will you do for a job?"

Elroy grinned shyly. "Find a job in a garage, or a track."

"Do you plan to race?"

"Yes." Elroy blushed. "If they'll let me."

"Hang on to your chair, Elroy," said Aggie. "I want to make you an offer. You don't really want to leave the ministry, do you?"

"No. But . . ."

"Just listen, and don't say anything 'till I'm finished."

††††††

The brisk Daytona wind tugged at the speeding racer, forced him to slow on the straightaway, sent him back to the pits after thirty minutes. "Too windy," he grunted. "But the bike's runnin great, Charlie."

"It orta be," growled the mechanic. "That's the third new motor this month. Don't you ever slow down?"

"Not unless I have to," laughed the rider.

†††††

"Well?" asked Aggie. "What do you think?"

"He's too big. A good racer is about five feet tall and 120 pounds." The portly, well dressed man shook his head. "He'll never win, Miss Patton."

"Mr. Case," Aggie said firmly. "We're not really talking about motorcycle races. We're talking souls."

"You're a hard woman, Aggie."

"That I am. How much, Mr. Case?"

He grinned. "Put us down for ten thousand. I'll see if the other sponsors and owners will chip in, too. Have you really put up all the money so far?"

Aggie nodded. "Sister and I. Our savings, and a mortgage."

"Why?"

Aggie smiled brightly. "Just call it faith, Mr. Case."

†††††

Elroy Wheelright showered, dressed, and stopped outside the camper to look again at the bright lettering on the side. He smiled.

"THE MOTORCYCLE MINISTRY." Below, in smaller print, was "Reverend Elroy Wheelright, racing for the greater glory of God."

Elroy sighed, and walked slowly toward the "church." His chapel was a tin shed, a converted garage, filled now with me-

chanics, riders, and other helpers from the busy racetrack.
Elroy nodded a greeting, took the podium, and lifted his
arms for the opening hymn. Aggie pumped the portable organ,
and the music swelled, echoing against the corrugated tin
roofing and spilling softly out across the soft darkness of the
deserted track.

††††††

A track security guard, drawn by the chorus of raspy voices,
walked closer and watched through a dusty window until his
radio crackled and ordered him to complete his rounds. At the
checkpoint the supervisor looked up from his supper and
frowned. "What's goin on down there?"

"It's the durndest thing," said the guard. "That preacher
feller—the one that races the Yamaha—he's got fifty people in
there for services."

"Hell, Walt," said the supervisor, "if they was ever a bunch
that needed prayin, this is it."

"Him and that little old woman, they go all over, preachin
and meetin with motorcycle people. Why you reckon he does
it?"

"Got a callin, I guess," grunted the supervisor. He grinned.
"But lemme tell you somethin, Walt. Come tomorrow, when
the race starts, Wheelright'll be right down there pushin and
shovin with the best of 'em. He may be a preacher, but he
wants to win as bad as anybody."

Walt sighed and stared off at the chapel. "Strange. Don't
he already know he's the biggest winner in the bunch?"

SWITCHBACK

His mother was a North Carolina Cherokee. His father, a four time state fiddling champion, was a leathery mountaineer with little patience with modern ways.

Kermit, youngest of the five sons, was a month old when his mother died. Jake Wheeler took the boys, the hounds, and his fiddle to a remote cabin in the Cherokee National Forest. He used the monthly forest service check to buy flour, coffee, ammunition and fiddle strings. He either grew, killed, or found everything else they needed. Kermit, fat and greasy, was free to eat any food that fell on the floor, and to sleep snuggled close to the big hounds. His playmates were the wild deer, fox, raccoon, and an infrequent Indian child. He carried his knife from the time he could walk, and carved his own toys from blocks of native hardwood.

Kermit was nine when Jake gave in, took his youngest to the barber shop and shoe store, and enrolled him in the county school. Kermit's knife silenced any ridicule, and even the teachers gave the mountain boy a wide berth. He was an indifferent scholar, able but given to daydreaming, and there were no objections when he did not return for the eighth grade.

Kermit was content in the Smokies, a restless wanderer and naturalist, but WW II jerked him from the forest. At nineteen he was a medical corpsman in Southern Italy. A shell destroyed the ambulance, and Kermit woke up after surgery to discover that his left leg was missing from the knee down. He was discharged in 1946, walking slowly but stubbornly erect on the wooden leg, and promptly threw the Purple Heart into the waters of the Oconoluftee River. He did cash the monthly disability checks.

In 1947, at the insistence of VA officials, Kermit took his GI Bill and enrolled in a Georgia vocational school, training to become a medical technician. He stayed two weeks. Back home, he used the remaining money to buy twenty acres on Wildwater Creek, at the head of the cove, and moved in a rusting mobile home.

The VA officials sent to collect the money from Kermit left hurridly, sped by visions of Kermit's flashing knife, and reported the funds as uncollectible.

In 1950 Kermit drove to Murphy and brought home a wife, a gap toothed mountain girl, deflowered her on the trailer floor and started the first of the seven babies.

Kermit supported his family by selling woodcarvings and hand made dulcimers, working sometimes as a game warden, and by playing music at folk festivals. When the wife demanded more money Kermit found her a job at the towel factory. When she complained, he broke her jaw and fled, spending two weeks hidden deep in the mountains. He came back, was met by a wary deputy with a warrant, and went quietly to the Cherokee County Jail. He was released in two weeks, came home and threw his wife into Wildwater Creek.

She crawled out, sputtering and swearing, sent for the sheriff, and Kermit left for Craggy Prison to serve two years. He had refused, during the trial, to talk; Kermit reckoned that a man did not discuss his personal problems in front of a crowd.

He was happy at Craggy. Kermit played music for the inmates, worked in the woodshop, oiled and cleaned the guards' rifles, and was free from his wife. She also stayed busy. Her eighth child was delivered during the second year of Kermit's imprisonment. He had no comment, but when he was paroled went deep into the hills to join Jake. Once a month, Kermit drove into Asheville to collect his government check and turn over half his earnings to the court for child support.

Jake's death forced Kermit out of the cabin. He lived in the back of his old station wagon until he found the remote cabin near Marshall, on the French Broad River, and moved in. He sat up his bandsaw in the living room, his cot in the back, and settled into his work. Kermit's fame as a folk musician and craftsman spread, and most evenings he was joined around the fire by groups of researchers, students, and fellow musicians.

One reporter came to visit and stayed.

Aggie, newly divorced from a New York stockbroker, parked her yellow Volvo close to the house to tape her interview with Kermit and never left. Kermit dutifully warned Aggie that he did not want any woman on a permanent basis. She laughed, agreed, and shared his cot.

When Kermit's wife delivered the ninth baby, he stopped taking the child support money to Asheville. In due time the court acted, and Deputy Jeb Harkins drove to the cove. Jeb found Kermit beside the fire, whittling, grinning.

"How do, Jeb," said Kermit. "I been expectin you."

He shifted slowly, rolled into a sitting position, and sat with his back close to the flames. Kermit, 55, was almost six feet tall, heavy bellied, and his thick hair was pulled straight back. His wool shirt was open halfway to his waist, and a droopy mustache accented his easy grin.

"Want some coffee, Jeb?" he asked. "I got plenty."

He reached for the tin pot, boiling over the ashes, and poured.

Jeb sipped gingerly, straining the grounds through clenched teeth. He sighed, and squatted close to Kermit. "I got papers, Kermit."

Kermit grinned. "Don't surprise me none, Jeb." He scratched an armpit, spat into the flames, and pondered. "I guess you want me to come with you."

"Yep." Jeb smiled. "Are ye goin to come?"

"Nope." Kermit opened his knife and cleaned his fingernails. "I ain't gonna go this time, Jeb." He inspected the sharp blade. "What are you goin to do?"

"I got to take you in," said Jeb.

"I told you. I ain't goin." Kermit grinned, and stared at Jeb.

The deputy drank his coffee and reconsidered. "Kermit," he finally said, "I need to run over to Marshall before I go back to Asheville. I could pick you up on my way back."

Kermit smiled slowly. "You do that, Jeb. Me and you, we go back a long ways."

Jeb frowned. "Reckon you could fix my Winchester while I'm gone?"

"Yep. Leave it. It'll be layin right here."

Jeb returned after two hours and found a worried Aggie. His .30-.30 was propped against the porch. "Aggie," he said softly, "I ain't seen hide ner hair of Kermit all day."

Jeb drove back to Asheville. "Couldn't find him nowheres," he told the sheriff. "I looked all over."

The sheriff grunted. "I'll send somebody back in the mornin. You reckon Kermit'll be at home?"

"I kinda doubt it, sheriff," said Jeb.

As he started out the door the sheriff stopped him. Jeb waited.

"Kermit fix your Winchester?" asked the sheriff. He grinned.

Jeb leaned against the doorjamb and smiled. "He shore did."

††††††

Kermit squatted on a rock above his Wildwater Cove trailer and watched.

A bleary, stumbling man left the trailer and drove toward the highway. He had spent the night inside, with Kermit's wife. The woman stood in the doorway, hands on her hips, watching him go. She stepped back inside, reappeared in minutes to throw empty beer bottles into the trash pile beside the door. A scrawny brown pup crawled out from under the trailer to sniff hungrily, and to nose through the new waste. The woman cackled, took careful aim, and smacked the pup's hindquarters with a savagely thrown bottle. The pup yelped, tried to run, and twisted to snap frantically at its dragging hindquarters.

The woman laughed and slammed the door as she went back inside.

Kermit bristled. "That done it," he growled. The slow climb down took him twenty minutes.

When Abe Williams returned, carrying a sack of groceries and a whiskey bottle, he found her draped across the trailer steps. A neat, circular cut ran from earlobe to earlobe, and the gummy blood was still dripping.

The sheriff was there in thirty minutes. "Ain't much doubt," he concluded gloomily. "Looks like Kermit's doins. She may have deserved it, but . . . we gotta go git Kermit, Jeb."

Jeb Harkins shivered and stared up at the green peaks. "They's near thirty thousand acres up yonder, sheriff," he said softly. "Findin Kermit ain't gonna be easy, and gittin him down . . ." He shuddered again. "He won't come alive, sheriff."

†††††

Kermit left the station wagon at the end of the fire trail, lifted the canvas sack and the crippled pup, and walked. The sack contained coffee, flour, condensed milk, a battered skillet and tin pot. In his pocket were extra cartridges and a heavy .44 Magnum.

The puppy, wrapped in an old wool shirt, whimpered and jerked, semi-conscious, and twice Kermit stopped to bring it water from the gurgling river. At dusk he found shelter under an overhang, built a fire and heated milk. The pup lapped greedily, licked his hand in mute appreciation, and they slept curled close together.

The morning sun woke Kermit. He saw a shadow and grabbed

for the revolver, and stopped short when he recognized Aggie, sitting crosslegged beside him, smiling. "How'd you git here?" asked Kermit.

"I followed you."

"Dang it." Kermit sat wearily. "Go on back, Aggie. Go on home."

"No." She leaned closer. "You killed her, didn't you? I heard, on the radio. I came to help, Kermit, and I'm staying with you."

Kermit sighed. "I done it, Aggie." He reached for the whimpering puppy.

"Who's your new friend?" asked Aggie. "Where'd you get him?"

Kermit grinned. "You might say I stoled him."

Aggie reached out. "No. Be careful," warned Kermit. "He's hurt pretty bad."

Aggie fed the pup while Kermit boiled coffee.

"Where are you goin?" she asked.

"Switchback Mountain." Kermit squinted into the sun, and peered up at the steep slopes. "Take about another day of walkin."

"They're after you," said Aggie. "The sheriff, the state police, the park rangers. Everybody."

"They won't find me." Kermit shouldered the sack, and Aggie reached for her pack. "What's in that?" he asked.

"Food. A first aid kit. Fishing line." Aggie smiled. "Your carving knives."

They walked upriver, always climbing, and in late afternoon reached the base of Switchback Mountain. After a night in a clearing they climbed higher, to the cave Kermit remembered. "It's got runnin water." He pointed to the spring. "And it's warm in the wintertime."

"I love it," said Aggie.

They set up their new home, and Kermit snared two rabbits to cook over the fire. The pup chewed a bone, and growled fiercely when Kermit teased him.

"He's lots better," laughed Aggie.

"Fierce, too," grunted Kermit. "I'm gonna call him Warrior."

††††††

A week later the helicopter pilot swooped lower to investigate. He reached quickly for his mike. "Chief," he said excitedly, "I've found Kermit's car, and another one. At the end of the fire trail over on East River."

"Good work, Charlie," said the radio. "We're on the way. You keep looking, and we'll call when we get there."

The chopper swung upriver, rotors throbbing.

Kermit, a mile from the cave, crouched in the underbrush and watched. The helicopter hovered, five hundred feet off the ground, above the waterfall. Warrior broke away and ran, yapping, crossed the clearing and chased the shadow. The pilot saw the dog, circled, and came lower to investigate.

Kermit sighed, and braced against a tree to steady the big pistol. He held his breath, squinted, and fired. He thumbed the hammer quickly, moved sideways, and fired again. The second shot found the fuel tank. The explosion sent Warrior scampering for safety, and the helicopter twirled slowly down, smoking, and plunged into the river at the base of the waterfall.

††††††

Jeb Harkins, at the wheel of the dusty jeep, parked close to Kermit's station wagon. "Call the chopper," ordered the sheriff.

"Mobile Two to Chopper Three. Come in, Charlie." Jeb waited, then tried again. "Come in, damnit, Charlie. This here is Jeb."

The sheriff cursed softly. "Where do you reckon he's gone

off to?"

"Beats me," grunted Jeb. "They sure ain't no place up in yonder a body'd want to go visit."

†††††††

The pair of black bears were sniffing, curious and a little scared. The female, less timid, licked at Charlie's leg.

"No, damn you!" he screamed. "Get away from me!"

The bear reared, growling, sniffed again and nuzzled closer.

"No!" Charlie died screaming, staring up at the bear as it ripped his leg apart at the knee.

†††††††

The sheriff scribbled busily. "The Volvo is registered to an Agatha Bronson, from Connecticut," he grunted.

"I mighta knowed," chuckled Jeb. "Kermit took 'im a good lookin woman along. Hell, sheriff, he's settin up there watchin us, all fat and sassy and dry."

The sheriff scowled. "Listen to me, Jeb. Kermit killed that woman. We ain't servin child support papers no more. Kermit killed once, and he ain't got nothin to lose by killin again. Especially if some damn fool deputy forgits to watch his-self."

Jeb gulped. "I hear you, sheriff."

The search parties fanned out, fighting their way upriver. An observation plane led them to the helicopter. A park service ranger stared bleakly. "Bear," he choked. "Or boar."

The young reporter from Asheville staggered to the bushes and was violently ill.

†††††††

Aggie huddled close to Kermit. "Are they here?"

"Close," he grunted. "But they ain't gonna find us."

"Kermit, don't go out any more. It scares me, while they're so close."

Kermit grinned. "I told you to go home."

"No." She clung to him. "I'm staying, but . . I'm afraid."

Warrior wedged his head between them. "Git, you damned dog," chuckled Kermit. "We got better things to do than play with you."

On the bed of leaves, high on Switchback Mountain, the baby was conceived.

†††††††

Heavy November snows blocked the search, grounded the planes, and the newspapers lost interest. "Besides," said the sheriff, "they ain't no way Kermit can last out the winter."

Jeb looked up from polishing his rifle. "Don't bet on that," he said quietly. "Kermit's half Indian, and now he's back where he growed up. He'll make it, sheriff."

†††††††

Warrior snuggled deep in the leaves and chewed busily on the splintered bone. Kermit had found the buck, trapped in a crevice, a week earlier. The coffee, flour, and sugar were gone, and now they lived on wild boar and the dried fruit Kermit had gathered in November. February winds blew the snow deep at the cave entrance, and bitter cold kept Kermit and Warrior inside except to hunt. A full beard warmed Kermit's face, and he lay flat by the fire, whittling. Aggie, her belly swelling, sat close by. The baby was due in early June.

Kermit stirred. "Aggie, you need milk, and vegetables, for the baby."

"No. I'm fine, Kermit."

He scowled into the flames. "I got to go to Cherokee," he

finally said.

"It's too dangerous," protested Aggie. "There's too much snow. You'll never make it."

"It's the best time," said Kermit. "They ain't gonna be lookin for me in this weather."

He wrapped himself in hides, tied Warrior to keep him from following, and left at mid morning. After three days Aggie lost hope, and prayed for a quick death. Resigned to fate and boars, she waited alone, close to the fire and Warrior.

The man who stomped into the cave, shaking off snow, wore a down parka, knee length boots and canvas mittens, and carried a carbine. He dragged in the sled.

"Want some supper?" asked Kermit.

Warrior barked happily, and danced across the cave.

Aggie, smiling, fainted.

Later, stuffed and warm, Aggie sorted the bounty. Milk— powdered and condensed, dried eggs, coffee, sardines, sugar, flour, tinned meat, canned fruit, and even chocolate filled the packs.

Kermit watched, sipping bourbon.

Aggie unrolled a down sleeping bag. "Kermit! How?"

"I went to Asheville."

Aggie froze. "To Asheville? Kermit, you could have been arrested."

"Wasn't nothin," said Kermit. "Jack Allison took me, and this beard covers me up good."

"Did you talk to anybody?"

"Just Jack. And he ain't gonna tell. Not no white man, nohow."

††††††

Spring brought flowery warmth to the Smokies, and Kermit picked plump fresh strawberries for Aggie. She spent hours, swollen breasts drooping, basking in the sunshine.

The baby came at dawn, in early June, and Kermit held him up for inspection. "Jake," he grinned. "After my daddy." Warrior crowded in to help clean the baby, and Aggie shrieked in dismay. "Leave him be," said Kermit. "Dogs is cleaner'n people." He held Jake and let the dog lick him clean.

Aggie wrinkled her nose and watched warily.

Kermit, who had spent little time with his other children, was with little Jake every day. He washed him in clear creek water, and carried him across the mountains to point out the different trees, flowers, and birds of Switchback. Aggie smiled. "He'll grow up wild."

"Just like his daddy," said Kermit.

"I hope so," said Aggie.

†††††

In Cherokee, Jack Allison was struggling with his conscience as he read of the reward for Kermit's capture. Kermit was Jack's half cousin, a close friend, a trusted fellow woodsman.

The reward was $5,000, more than Jack had ever hoped to see at one time, and he made his choice. As they drove toward Asheville he explained to his wife. "Kermit," grunted Jack, "he's just half Indian, anyhow."

Jeb Harkins watched Jack Allison leave, and kicked the wall in angry disgust.

"Jeb?" The other deputy stood clear. "Are you gonna tell the sheriff?"

"I am, damnit," snapped Jeb. "In a minute."

"You and Kermit, you was friends, wasn't you?"

"We was." Jeb sighed. "But it looks like Kermit's friends is goin fast." He made the call, and the sheriff ordered the full scale manhunt.

†††††

At the foot of Switchback Mountain Jeb found the traps. "Kermit's," he said softly. "Rabbit snares."

The others gathered to peer at the first evidence that Jack Allison had told the truth. The men squirmed nervously, alert to every sound, eyes on the slopes. From a hundred yards away Kermit watched calmly, then retreated to the cave. Aggie was nursing Jake.

"Are they here?" she asked.

Kermit tied Warrior, his face grim and cold, and turned. "Just down the mountain, Aggie. I got to go, tonight." He hesitated. "It'd be safer if you was to go to 'em, Aggie. You and little Jake."

"No," said Aggie. "We're staying with you, Kermit. No matter what."

Kermit stared at her serious expression. "Hell, Aggie," he chuckled. "You done turned into a mountain woman."

They waited, speaking little. Kermit packed their gear, then took time to clean and load his weapons. Aggie watched, solemn.

"Would you really shoot? If they get close?"

Kermit nodded. "If I have to. I ain't goin back."

Warrior whimpered and pressed close to little Jake.

By dusk the search party was halfway up the mountain. They stopped to pitch tents, set up a communications center, built cooking fires, and posted sentries. Almost fifty men, all heavily armed and edgy, slept uneasily.

In the cave Kermit gently petted Warrior.

"He can't go with us," he said softly.

Aggie's eyes widened. "But what . . .?"

"Wait outside," Kermit ordered. His voice was thick with emotion.

When he joined Aggie his face was wet. "Let's go," he said quickly. "Be quiet, and follow me."

††††††

"Damn!" The deputy staggered back from the cave entrance. "They's a big dog, dead." He stumbled out into the
bright sunlight. "Somebody cut it's throat."

They found the sleeping bags and cooking utensils. "Kermit
wintered here," confirmed Jeb. "Jack was right. Kermit and the
girl was both here. He's killed the dog so it wouldn't give him
away."

"Where is he now?" asked the sheriff.

Jeb squinted. "Either up on top," he said, "or he slipped
down past us last night. My guess is down."

"We'll go both ways," said the sheriff. "Jeb, you go down.
Take half the men. I'll take the rest and check out the top.
We'll join you if we don't find anything. Stay in touch by
radio." He paused, and took a deep breath. "I don't reckon I
have to tell you to be careful. Kermit ain't gonna be happy to
see us."

Jeb nodded glumly. "Jack give Kermit a big old deer rifle,
last winter."

††††††

Kermit struggled with the rifle, pack and baby, but at mid-
afternoon Aggie collapsed. "I just can't go on," she gasped.
"Leave us here, Kermit. You go on. You can come back for us
later."

"Set a while," Kermit said softly. He climbed up a rock to
peer back down the valley. "Damn," he whispered. "They're
here, already."

Jeb had led his party swiftly, following Kermit's trail of dis-
lodged rocks and twisted limbs, and was halfway across the
clearing when Kermit fired. Jeb's hat flew off crookedly, and
he fell flat and rolled for cover.

"Jeb?" Kermit's voice echoed.

Jeb lifted his head. "Yep. That you, Kermit?"

"Back off, Jeb," yelled Kermit. "I don't want to have to hurt none of you."

"We can't do that," answered Jeb. "You got to come with us, Kermit. Hell, you can't get away now. Don't be dumb and get somebody shot."

A trooper eased forward, and for a brief second showed himself. The bullet shattered the limb beside him.

"That's the last warnin," yelled Kermit. "From now on I'm shootin for keeps. Git 'em away from here, Jeb."

Jeb was on the radio, talking fast. "We found him, sheriff. I can talk him out, if you can hold off a while."

"I'm on my way," said the sheriff. "Talk if you want to, Jeb, but don't let him get away."

The anxious troopers stopped the talking. Twice, Kermit's accurate shooting sent them scrambling, one with a shattered wrist, and Jeb scowled. "He ain't tryin. If he was, you'd both be dead. You fellers let me do the talkin, we'll git Kermit outa there without anybody gittin hurt."

"It's too damn late for talkin, Jeb," said the sheriff. His men fanned out, circling. "Come dark, Kermit'll run for it. We'll take him then, however we have to."

†††††

Kermit was firm. "You take Jake," he told Aggie. "Go on with them. I don't want either one of you to get hurt. It's me they want."

"Come with us," pleaded Aggie.

"No," grunted Kermit. "I can't. I'll slip away and come back for you when I can."

"Promise?"

"I promise, Aggie." Kermit hesitated. "Go on, now."

†††††

The nervous searchers listened closely. "Over there," whispered a ranger. "Hear that?"

"Somebody comin," said Jeb. "Don't shoot."

A twig snapped, and a deputy fired. "No!" screamed Jeb. Rifles were roaring, and a shrill scream split the darkness. There was an uneasy silence as the search party moved closer, guns ready.

A ranger, first to the scene, sagged to feet. "My God," he whispered. "What have we done?"

Jeb broke through the thicket. "Lord help us, Jeb," sobbed the ranger. "We killed a woman and a baby."

Aggie's torn body was sprawled over a low limb, and the baby was close by. Jeb sunk to his knees.

Kermit, a half mile upstream, heard the gunfire and ran, cursing, stumbling and crying and charging directly into the cluster of stunned men.

†††††

The trooper was silent and bowed, comforting the two wounded men stretched across the clearing. A bleeding deputy spoke hoarsely. "He come outa the dark, yellin'" he gasped. "Like some kind of animal. We never had a chance."

"Get him out of here," ordered the sheriff. "How bad is it, Jeb?"

"Five dead," said Jeb. His vacant eyes reflected the moonlight. "Three of ours. Sheriff, we killed Kermit's son and his woman."

"Jeb, that's the least of your worries right now." The sheriff stood warily, pistol drawn. "Because right now, all because some trigger happy bastard couldn't wait, Kermit is huntin *us.*"

Jeb stared blankly. "Sheriff," he whispered, "Can you blame him?"

†††††

Wounded, dragging his splintered wooden leg, Kermit clung to the mossy rocks and climbed. His breath came in great, ragged gulps. On top of a ledge he rested, used his belt to strap the leg, and reloaded. He had seven rounds for the revolver, five for the rifle. He rested, then started down, back toward the camp and the search party.

The first sentry died quietly in the gurgle of his own blood.

Two more stood together, smoking and whispering. One died instantly, Kermit's blade buried in his chest. The other ran, screaming, and was shot in the back. Kermit retreated, hid, and waited calmly for daybreak and a final revenge.

No one slept, and when the gray dawn finally came the hunters stirred quietly. The sheriff stood to stretch and yawn. "Git down," hissed Jeb.

He was too late. From four hundred yards Kermit's aim was true. The sheriff snorted, toppled into the laurel, and died with his yawn half finished.

Beating helicopter rotors signalled relief from the siege. Kermit aimed, then lowered the rifle. The two choppers skimmed low over the trees, snipers ready in the doors, and Kermit retreated.

The gun crews were operating under the directive they had received at dawn from the governor. "Find Kermit Wheeler and kill the son of a bitch!"

††††††

Sore, dizzy, Kermit pressed closer to the face of the cliff and watched the troopers climb slowly closer. He bent, aimed, fired, and the lead man fell. The others retreated, and the helicopters swung closer, pinning Kermit in the ravine.

"We got him," said Jeb. "Not even Kermit Wheeler can get outa there."

"Then lets finish him off," snarled the state police captain.

"Wait him out," advised Jeb. "He can't stay in there forever, and he can't escape. Save a lot of shootin, captain."

"You can wait," growled the captain. He reached for his radio. "Move in," he ordered.

Another trooper fell, and the party was trapped by Kermit's fire. "Damn," said the captain. "We'll blow him out." He ordered the waiting forest service tanker plane into position, and guided the pilot by radio. The plane dived, dropped its load of chemical, and peeled away. The following helicopter moved in, and a gunner dropped two explosive charges.

††††††

The foul liquid drenched Kermit, flushed him away from the cliff, and then the explosions lifted him into the air. He soared, arms flailing, crashed to a rock below, and his rifle clattered to the cliff base. Kermit lay prone, stiff, draped across a ledge in the sunlight.

"That got him, by damn," growled the captain.

Jeb stared. His fists were clenched, and his lip trembled. "Do you all think you can handle Kermit now?" he asked softly. "Or have you got the Marines comin in next?" He spat and walked away, climbing.

"Where do you think you're going?" yelled the captain.

Jeb squinted, and looked down at the trooper. "If it's okay by you, captain, I'm goin to git Kermit. What little's left of him."

The officer glared, started to speak, then grinned. "What the hell? You go on and do the cleaning up for us, deputy."

††††††

Kermit clenched the pistol. Flies buzzed around his wounds, and his head swirled. He waited, determined to make good use of his final shot.

"Kermit?" Jeb's soft voice came from the brush. "Are you

there, Kermit?"

"Yeah. Over here, Jeb."

Jeb crawled closer. "I thought you was dead, old buddy," he said softly.

"I am," croaked Kermit.

"Nope. Hang on, Kermit, and I'll git you down from here."

"I can't go, Jeb," whispered Kermit. He lifted the revolver. Jeb stared down the barrel of the big .44 magnum.

††††††

Below, the sharpshooter was ready. He focused, matched the crosshairs with Kermit's forehead, and waited.

††††††

"Go on, Kermit," said Jeb. "Git it over with."

Kermit chuckled, his throat rattling. "Hell, Jeb," he gasped. "You know I wouldn't hurt a friend."

He dropped the pistol, and Jeb scooted closer.

††††††

The captain smiled. "Fire," he snapped.

The high velocity bullet shattered Kermit's skull, blowing a mist of blood and bone across Jeb's face. Kermit's body twitched, rolled, and slid off the ledge. Jeb crawled to look down, then lay flat, pounding the rock with his fists and sobbing.

The rescue crew battled fallen timbers and tangled laurel, steep outcroppings and a blazing sun, and in an hour were close to Kermit's body. From behind the thicket came grunting noises, growing louder, and the team leader drew his pistol. He crept forward, hammer pulled, breath frozen. He peered through the brush, and gasped as he met Kermit Wheeler's lopsided grin.

Then he screamed, jerked the trigger, and fell backwards away from the clearing.

The frenzied wild boar, blood dripping, squealed and crashed through the brush, away from the tangled remains and the very sick crew leader.

††††††

From the ledge Jeb watched, and his laughter suddenly rang from the mountainside, a maniacal cackle of relief and revenge, and when his breath was gone he slumped to the rocks and wept.

THE REUNION

She lay, breathing with difficulty, in the hard hospital bed.

Eva Davis was 83. She stood—or had for 70 years—an inch short of five feet, and weighed 82 pounds, down from her life-long 102. Her hair was white cornsilk, pulled and braided, tied into a small knot at the back of her head. She wore a loose fitting hospital gown, blue stripes on faded white, tied behind her neck.

A plastic IV bottle dripped nourishment and antibiotics into a vein of her left forearm, and curling tubes through her nostrils cleared her lungs.

Eva was dying.

Diabetes, kept at bay for 35 years, now poisoned the extremities of her body. In her left leg there was gangreen, painful and fatal; in the largest artery of her neck a thickening clot hung ready to move to her brain.

An hour earlier the apologetic young surgeon, halting and reluctant, had told her. "Mrs. Davis, we have to . . . remove . . . your leg. Above the knee. If we don't . . . you'll . . . you'll be dead in a week.

"Don't ye be worryin'," she had told him. "I knowed. From the hurtin. Hit's the gangreen, haint it?"

"Yes." He was quiet. "It's . . too far gone."

"Then take 'er," she said. "You know best."

"There . . . there's more." He swallowed. "Mrs. Davis, if we operate there's a chance you'll . . . that you won't live. The blood clot may move. If it does . . . " He shrugged. "It's a 50-50 chance. You may die, Mrs. Davis."

"I thank ye, doctor." She appraised the young surgeon, and was pleased. "You do it, yerself. Nobody else. Don't let no strangers go cuttin on me."

"I won't." He smiled. "I'll do my best, Mrs. Davis."

"I know ye will." She looked into his eyes. "When?"

"Tomorrow. Early in the morning."

He had gone, white jacket swirling.

Evie was left alone, except for 83 years of memories.

††††††

She tugged at the handle, and the blade dug in and stuck tighter.

"Evie, God Damnit," growled Mark, "Don't lean on it. Pull, up to ye, and easy."

She did, and the crosscut saw slipped smoothly through the hickory log. Evie staggered, and hung on to the handle.

"Leggo," he yelled. "Don't lean on the durn thing, Evie! Hell's Bells woman! Ain't you ever goin to learn?"

"I'm a doin my best, Mark." Tears ran softly. "Don't go yellin at me." The large, soft brown eyes clouded. "I never done nothin like this afore."

He blew out a whistling breath, and finally grinned. "I know it," he said. "Little bit of a woman like you, I can't expect ye to go whuppin a big ol' saw. But Evie, iffen ye'd jist quit tryin so hard! It'll work, if ye'll go easy. Quit pushin and leanin. Jis pull, up and easy, atter I let go. Don't ride it, Evie."

She wiped her eyes, spat on her hands, and tugged at the saw. "C'mon, you son of a bitch," she whispered. "Saw, Damnit!"

"Ease up!" yelled Mark.

Evie shrugged, pulled lightly, and—to her amazement— slid the teeth of the crosscut smoothly across the log. "It works," she yelled, dropping the saw and dancing with joy. "It worked, Mark!"

Mark leaned on the saw, spat a brown stream of tobacco

juice, and grinned.

Evie, 14 and married for nearly a year, giggled. She was a curious half child, half woman, likely to play with her dolls for an hour before she crawled into the bed to make passionate love to her 23 year old husband.

"Evie, ain't you never worked?"

"Jis in the house," she replied angrily. "We was never so poor that the wimmin had to do man's work." She jerked up her skirts, leaped over the log, dancing lightly as she landed, and stuck out her tongue. "So there, Mark Davis! You didn't marry no trash."

He laughed, and the sounds rang from the frosty October hillsides.

††††††

She muttered in her half sleep, legs jerking in memory of Octobers past.

"Mamma?" Through the fog she heard him. Kenneth, sweet little Kenneth. The oldest, born in the big blizzard.

"Mamma?" The sound echoed, drumming across her brain.

"Kenneth. My baby." Her voice, cracking and slurred, strained as she focused. "That you, Kenneth?"

"I'm here, Mamma." He loomed over her, almost frightening in his bulk. A thick arm swung closer, and the cool, strong hand clasped her wrist. "How are you, Mamma?"

††††††

She remembered, perfectly, his first sounds.

It was February, 1912. The heaviest snows in memory, and bitter cold, lashed at the Davis cabin. Wind howled up through the floor, and icy snow filtered under the door.

Evie struggled against the cold, feeding the fire and shivering under the winter quilts, her bulky belly making her awkward.

Mark had left the day before, bundled against the cold, promising to return with the midwife before dark. Her supply of firewood was dangerously low. The pains, fierce and stabbing, were coming more often.

She dragged her mother's old wool coat from the bench and buttoned it tight. She hesitated at the door, then plunged out into the howling wind.

She screamed at the sudden pain, the biting cold. The woodpile, 20 yards away, was barely visible in the blowing snow. Six trips. Two logs per trip. She dropped the logs, stripped off the icy boots, and thrust her fingers to the fire. In time she added the four biggest logs to the grate, and spread sheets and quilts before the fireplace.

Kenneth's angry squalls broke the frigid silence. Evie cleaned him, added the last logs to the fire, and sat patiently, wrapped in the gay quilts.

The wood was gone at dawn.

At dusk, Mark found her, blankets open to warm the suckling baby against her breasts.

†††††††

"Kenneth, hit's you, ain't it?"

"I'm here, Mamma."

Kenneth moved slowly, crippled by arthritis and years of backbreaking labor. "Mark, he's here too, and Michael and Sammy." Three generations of Davis men hovered, surrounding the little bed, blocking the feeble light. "The others is out in the hall, Mamma."

Evie Davis had borne 11 children, and 10 still lived. There were **74 grandchildren** and **139 great-grandchildren**. "The others" referred simply to the children, drawn together from far and wide, gathered to offer comfort to the small, dying woman.

"They all here?"

"Ever one, Mamma."
The youngest, Dean, had been born in 1932.

††††††

"Again?" Mark's jaw dropped. "Damnit, Evie, I wish I could git the cows on as reglar a schedule as you're on."

Evie smiled. "Them cows ain't got you atter 'em ever night," she said. "They jis git chased down onct a year."

"I mind the last baby," said Mark, suddenly gloomy.

"She wasn't meant to live, Mark," said Evie. "This un'll be fine."

He was. The nine pound boy, the last born in the big canopy bed, was a lusty and hungry baby.

But Evie did not fare well. Phlebitis—"milk leg"—set in, and her left leg shriveled. The pain kept Evie in the bed for over six months, and well over a year had passed before she walked normally.

"No more, Evie," decreed Mark. "Yer through havin babies. Anothern would kill ye."

"Well," she said, "Dean, he'll jis have to keep on bein the baby."

††††††

The visitors were gone, and the drugs fogged Evie's mind. She was not sure. The young man, gone now, had talked about a funeral home. She had told him Miller's in Westville. The Davises were Miller's people, and had been for over 50 years.

"Are you sure?" he had asked, a strange look on his face.

"Yes. I'm sure." Evie had insisted. She spurned his questioning look, and sent him scurrying from her room.

Miller's was a fine funeral home. Evie knew.

It was February, 1968. Evie stood before the kitchen window and watched as Kenneth walked slowly from his car. His face, a solemn mask, told her the news.

She met him at the door. "Hit's Mark, ain't it?"

"Yes." He was quiet. "Daddy's dead. He fell, over by the crick." He clenched his large fists. "Damn, I told 'im, a thousand times! He was too old to be runnin with them dogs. I told 'im, Mamma." He sobbed softly.

Evie held the large, trembling hands. "Your daddy," she said, "He didn't want to die in no bed. Hit's best this way, son." She knotted her hands in the apron. "Where is he? I got to go to him."

"Miller's," said Kenneth. "They just picked him up. Mamma, it'll be a while . . . fore you can . . . see 'im."

He choked. "And I . . . I got to git some clothes fer 'im."

"I'll do it," said Evie. In their bedroom she laid out Mark Davis' black suit—"fer marryin and buryin"—and clean, starch-ed underwear, his newest shoes, and a stiff rarely used blue tie.

"Take these on," she said, "I'll be bakin. We'll be needin food, fer the family, and I'll be gittin it ready."

"Mamma," said Kenneth. "Come with me. To my place."

"No," she said calmly, "I'll be stayin here."

Then I'll have Dean come by and stay with you and bring you to the funeral home later."

In Miller's Funeral Home the family gathered. Those living in Ohio were enroute, due to arrive during the night. Those close by were already there, smoking and milling, still in a state of shock, almost angry at their father's sudden death.

"Where's he at?" asked Evie.

"This way, Miz Davis," said George Miller. He took her arm and led her into a dimly lit, ornately trimmed carpeted sanctuary.

Evie stared, for a long time, remembering.

"You done a good job, George. You allys do."

"Thank ye, Miz Davis. He was a fine man, Mark was."

✝✝✝✝✝✝

Evie tossed in her stupor.

The young surgeon was over her, feeling for her pulse.

"It's almost time," he said, "How do you feel?"

"Is it mornin?"

He smiled. "Sure is. See you in a few minutes, Mrs. Davis."

He was gone, and a stream of attendants came and left, administering shots and pills, offering assurance, thoroughly confusing Evie.

The last one asked for her teeth and wedding ring.

"Why, no," she mumbled. "Ye ain't gittin 'em. This ring, hit ain't been offen my finger fer 70 year. Ye ain't gittin it. Ner my teeth, neither."

Kenneth's voice swam in from somewhere. "They have to, Mamma. You'll get 'em back."

"No!" she screamed. Or she thought she screamed.

✝✝✝✝✝✝

Evie was back, roaming the fields, her old dog Rex leaping playfully beside her, the sleepy white mare grazing in the tall weeds. Below her was the cabin, morning glories vining up the walls, and her mother was sweeping the porch, laughing at the antics of her brother Bob and the tumbling puppies.

"Mamma!" she yelled, "I'm here. It's me, Evie. I'm comin, Mamma." She ran, skipping across the dusty earth, barely skimming the ground.

✝✝✝✝✝✝

"Mrs. Davis!" The harsh command jarred her ears. "Wake up!"

"I'm awake." Her voice trembled.

She was on her back, moving rapidly, lights flashing over-head, voices rumbling, and then was lifted, dropped, down and down and down and . . .

"Mamma? Mamma?"

It was Kenneth, clasping her hand.

"You're OK, Mamma," he said through the drumming. "It's all over."

"My . . . my leg . . . it hurts, Kenneth . . . " She groaned, and was swept back into the swimming void.

††††††

"Are you sure?" Earl Miller paced the floor. "I mean, layin out bodies is one thing. But a leg?"

"Earl, that's what she wants." Dean kicked at the carpet. "That's what mommy wants, damnit." He stood and licked his lips. "It's what she told 'em, last night, and got madder'n hell. Do it! Bury the leg, Earl."

Earl sighed. "I'll take it, Dean. And I'll put it in a box. But I ain't buryin no leg! Do it yerself."

"OK," said Dean. "Just git it ready. I'll do it."

Earl stepped to the door. "Ya'll crazy, ye know?"

"Just do it, Earl. Just do it, God Damn it!"

††††††

It was an infant's coffin, small and blue and feminine. Earl snapped the lid shut, and shuddered. Dean Davis waited.

"It's done," he told him.

"Well, help me load it, Earl."

"You gonna drive right through town? With that thing there layin in the back?"

"Got to, Earl."

"Then, by God, let's at least put a blanket over it."

Dean dug a hole in the corner of the family plot, small and deep. He unloaded the casket. "Damn iffin I know," he said to himself, "if this calls fer prayin and preachin."

With a pair of ropes he lowered the small coffin, and quickly shoveled in the loose dirt and left.

††††††

Evie was home, at Dean's, a month later. He carried her to the house, sat her gently on the sofa, and grinned.

"Mommy," he said, "You don't weigh as much as a good sized hound puppy."

Kenneth arrived after Evie had been positioned, resting against a pillow and covered by one of her own quilts. He carried a pair of aluminum crutches.

"'Jis throw 'em out," said Evie, "cause I ain't usin 'em."

"Now, looky here, Mamma," said Kenneth. "You're gonna be up walkin—on these—in a week er two. Then we'll git ye a leg."

"A wooden leg?"

"Yeah. "Cept now they're plastic." Kenneth grinned.

"It hurts," said Evie. "My leg, It ain't there, but it hurts."

"I know. They said it'd be like that." Kenneth gently patted her shoulder. "You surprised 'em. They said you was gonna die, Mamma."

"I knowed it," said Evie. "The night before, they was in there askin me which funeral home to call, and sich. To bury me, iffen I died."

Dean spat hot coffee across the floor.

"Mamma? They was askin? About buryin?"

"I don't member so good," said Evie, twisting, "They ast me, and I tol 'em Miller's. They was kinda quare actin, though, when I tol 'em. About Miller's. Like they was thinkin Miller's wasn't good enough. I had to git mean. I told 'em, I did, that Miller's been buryin us Davises about 50 year."

"Mamma?" Dean twisted his hands and chewed on his lip. "Did they—ask you—what to do with your leg?"

"What about it? They tooken it."

"Did they ast ye what ye wanted done with it? The stub? Er whatever it's called?"

"Now, Dean," blustered Kenneth,"They ain't no use in talkin about that."

"Hell they ain't!" yelled Dean.

"They burn 'em, I reckon," said Evie. "Hit don't make no matter to me."

Dean paled, and walked to his desk.

"Here." He thrust an envelope at Kenneth.

"Miller's? $450? What the hell for, Dean?"

††††††

"I didn't know what else to do," said Dean, as they stood by the small square of freshly turned earth. "They told me that's what she wanted. I didn't tell nobody."

"It in a casket?" asked Kenneth.

"Yep." Dean kicked at the red clods. "A baby's."

Kenneth's laugh started as a belly chuckle. It climbed, amplified, and burst out across the hilltop into pealing, ringing roars. Dean shuffled, grinned, then gave in.

Back at the house Evie was curious. "I heared the two of ye," she said, "a laughin, and a yellin. All the way down here. What was it?"

Dean blushed. "Mamma," he said, "I don't know how to tell ye this. They thought—at the hospital, fore the operation—you wanted to keep your leg. To bury. So I took it, and it's up on the hill."

"My leg?"

"Yeah." Dean shrugged. "I didn't know; they said that's what you wanted."

"You jus—throw it in a hole?"

"Hell, no." Dean laughed. "It's got it's own little casket, a blue one."

"Law." Evie sat, stunned. "Where'd you put it?"

"Over in . . . in the corner, Mommy. I didn't know. Hell, I never buried no leg before."

"Reckon nobody never." Evie smiled, weary and accepting. "I never heerd o' sich. Does George Miller know? What you and Earl done?"

"Hell, no. We never told 'im."

"Did youns put up a marker?"

"Fer a leg? What's it supposed to say? 'Here lies Evie Davis' leg, they cut it off?' "

"Now stop it, Dean," said Kenneth.

"Leave 'im be." Evie cackled. "I reckon I'd want to see. Where ye put it, and all."

"Oh, no," protested Kenneth, "You'll do no such thing."

"Hit's mine, ain't it?"

"Hell, " said Dean, "It's mine. Cost me $450."

Laughter drew tears to Evie's eyes.

"Dean, hit's yourn by rights. Hit's the same one got bad when you were borned. Hit's right, you payin fer it."

✝✝✝✝✝✝

"Oh, no," said Earl Miller. "Dean, I ain't gonna do it. I ain't, it don't matter what you say, I ain't. I ain't goin to, by God, and that's that!"

"I'll git it. And bring it here."

"Earl, it's what she wanted. For two year, now. She said to. You got to, Earl."

"No. I jis can't, Dean. I can't do her."

"Earl, God Damnit, you got to!"

Earl wavered. "You promise not to tell? Never?"

"Nobody," swore Dean. "Only ones'll know is us. And her." He grinned. "She'll know."

"Alright. I'll do it. Atter dark, though."

At midnight the steady, digging noises were muted by the heavy air. There were grunts and curses, and the clink of metal on metal. Then, the truck drove slowly away. At the mortuary, Earl took a deep breath.

††††††

"I'm comin, Mamma." She ran free, bouncing, dancing with delight. Down the hill, over the split rail fence, past the woodpile, across the garden. "I'm here, Mamma. I'm home."

††††††

The family passed Evie's coffin in a somber procession, led by Kenneth's shuffling, and tears flowed freely.

Dean Davis, with his wife and children, walked to the open coffin. Through the tears he grinned, and Earl Miller, catching his eye, looked at the floor.

††††††

Under the draped velvet, draped in soft white cotton, Evie Davis' leg lay snugly rejoined to her body.

THE HUNTERS

Buck Hamilton moved silently, slicing through the gray dawn, eyes alert and rifle ready. He stopped, cupped his hand to listen, and edged closer to the clearing. He leaned against a big hickory, pulled his cap low to block the first rays of the sun, and waited.

The chattering and chewing resumed. Buck squinted, tightened his finger over the cold trigger, and pressed his cheek against wet metal as he sighted. The swift crack of the .22 echoed lightly. There was a frenzy in the upper branches of the oak tree, then the squirrel dropped, spinning limply, falling to the damp grass.

Buck grinned, broke cover to claim his prey, stuffed the squirrel into a big game pocket, and whistled as he tramped homeward. He was there before breakfast, cleaned the carcasses and fed the entrails to the hounds, and carried the dressed meat into the house.

"Got four this mornin," he grunted. "Make us a good supper." He washed quickly, poured hot coffee, and sat at the table. "Is Billy up yet? I asked him to go with me, but he didn't want to."

"Billy's still asleep." Annie Hamilton sneaked a look at Buck, but stayed busy at the stove. "Buck, you're not goin to start on him again, are you? About huntin?"

Buck sighed. "I reckon not, Annie. I'm about to give up. The boy's plumb scared to death of guns."

"He's not scared," protested Annie, "he's just . . ."

"Billy's still your baby." Buck shook his head sadly. "Him

twelve years old. Annie, when I was Billy's age I was runnin my own trap line over on Bigger Creek, sellin hides and helpin feed the family. Me and pap'd keep fresh meat on the table all winter."

"Times has changed," Annie said softly. "Billy just don't like huntin and killin."

"He's a danged sissie," growled Buck. "A man ain't a man what can't shoot and handle hisself in the woods."

"Billy's not a man," said Annie. "He's still a little boy, Buck."

"It ain't right," Buck muttered darkly. "Me, of all people, raisin a boy what's scared of his own shadow." He stood, scowling. "I'm goin on to work." Buck found his heavy lunch pail, pulled on a mackinaw coat and fur lined cap, and stepped back outside. He stopped on the doorstep to survey his little homestead, swelling with pride at the fruits of his labor and his determination to rear his family in the country, well away from the crowded subdivisions and stacked apartment complexes.

Buck Hamilton's fifty acres lay ten miles east of Bakersville, at the base of Boone Mountain. He was surrounded by three thousand acres of ridgetops and scrub timber, land too steep for farming and too barren for mining. It was the Bakersville watershed, a deserted acreage which fed cold, clear water into a sixty acre lake and which served as a hunting preserve for Buck and other men of similar yearnings.

The Hamilton place was immaculate, with outbuildings painted to match the house and grounds trimmed to orderly precision. Winter firewood was cut and drystacked, hay for the mare and pony filled the barn, and the corncrib bulged. Two hogs were being fattened in their pen, a flock of chickens provided fresh daily eggs, and the milk cow huddled close to the barn for warmth. There were bees, four hives near the orchard, a sturdy grape arbor, and a fieldstone smokehouse filled with hams.

Buck, a lathe operator in Bakersville, earned more than

enough to have purchased one of the split levels in Country Estates. He stubbornly resisted, insisting that his children be reared with fresh air, room to grow, and the responsibilities of farm living.

Buck was one of eleven children, son of a hillside tenant farmer, a hunter and trapper and self sufficient scavenger. From the time he could remember, Buck had worked the mules to put in crops of corn and tobacco, buried potatoes in the straw lined pit, butchered hogs in the fall, manned one end of a busy crosscut saw, swung the double bitted axe, helped scratch a meager livelihood from seventy barren acres.

He was born to the forest, to the rifle, a native woodsman. Wild game was free food; hunting was recreation. Buck had slept under a gun rack, a proud display of well oiled rifles and shotguns, working tools of a rural family.

Buck was a Marine sharpshooter at seventeen. Back home, at 21, he went to the factory, and after two decades he was a model employee, a diligent craftsman and a steady producer. He had bought the farm the year Billy was born. When the boy was a month old Buck brought home the single shot .22, and at four Billy could break bottles from fifty yards, squealing with delight when his aim was true.

†††††††

"Maybe I rushed the boy," grunted Buck.

He climbed into his truck, a tough 4WD that doubled as farm wagon and transportation, and backed out carefully to miss the green sedan parked close by. He grinned. Beth, his fourteen year old daughter, was sneaking the car up and down the gravel driveway, practicing for a driver's license that was still two years away. Buck chuckled. His awkward daughter, half baby and half boy and half woman, was a leggy teenager who could flip from tough farm laborer to precocious sexpot with a twisting smile, who could help clean the rabbits then sob over a TV soap opera.

"*She* would make one hell of a man," grinned Buck.

Billy, five years ago, had balked at learning to hunt. The boy preferred to play with friends from the school, and he complained bitterly about his chores. Billy scorned the pony for a bicycle, the mare for a sputtering mini-bike, and the little .22 was rusting in a closet. The boy did not like Buck's hounds, and for a pet took a white kitten from the barn.

Buck frowned, wheeled the truck down the lane, and watched the fog lift from the mountain. After work, he decided, he'd hunt the south slope, down by the lake.

†††††

The following spring Buck worked late every evening, coming home from his factory shift to plow and plant, running the tractor well into the night to finish the job. This day, at dusk, he stopped the tractor near the fencerow to rest and smoke, and company came.

Two baby squirrels fussed from a low hanging limb, noisy and frantic. Buck swung down from the tractor, walked closer, and reached a big hand up to the branches. One baby squirrel ran quickly down his arm, up his shoulder, and snuggled under his collar.

"Doggone," chuckled Buck. "I ain't your mammy, little feller."

The other squirrel watched, chattering, leaping from limb to limb. "You want to come too?" Buck offered his arm and the second squirrel scampered to the warmth of his neck. Smiling, he carried them home to Beth.

"Orphans, I'd reckon," he told her. "Git a eyedropper and feed 'em, if you want to. They'd make good pets, least 'till they grow up and get mean."

Beth was delighted. She fixed a warm bed in a shoebox, and mixed milk and honey. The squirrels sucked greedily.

"Look, daddy!" Beth suddenly wailed. "They don't have any ears. Nothing sticks up."

Buck gently inspected the squirrels. "That's why they were alone," he said. "Their mother left them to die. Animals can tell, and they leave the defective young ones."

"That's awful." Beth shuddered.

"It's nature's way," Buck said softly. "Survival of the fittest."

"These two won't die," snapped Beth. "*I'll* be their mother."

She was. The squirrels, dubbed "Tom" and "Jerry," thrived under her care, graduating quickly from milk to peanuts, spilling out of the box and scampering wildly through the house. They terrorized Billy's cat, leaping and chattering and chasing, fussed at Annie in the kitchen, roughhoused with Beth and slept in a cage under her bed.

Buck remained a special friend to Tom and Jerry. As he sat, reading the paper after supper, the squirrels would perch on his shoulders, tails switching, seriously studying the paper and waiting for an opportunity to snuggle close against his neck.

"They know you saved them," giggled Beth. "You're their father."

Buck blushed, but he looked forward to seeing the squirrels every evening. Tom and Jerry grew rapidly, and by mid-summer were beginning to venture outside. They were cautious at first, staying high in the trees, fussing at the hounds. The big Walker dogs knew; they would not harm a family pet, and in time the squirrels had the run of the yard and the barn. Gradually they explored the hillside, but always came scratching at the door for food and the safety of the cage.

Buck warned Beth. "Pretty soon they'll leave, honey. To find mates, and build dens."

"Will other squirrels like them?" Beth was serious. "I mean Tom and Jerry not having ears. Can they find wives?"

Buck laughed. "I reckon they will, somehow. Maybe girl squirrels don't look too close."

Eventually both squirrels spent more and more time outside, and Tom was the first to spend the night away from home. Beth paced and worried, and Buck slept uneasily. But, at dawn, the scratching at the door signalled the adventurer's return. Both Tom and Jerry moved out, returning on occasion for food and petting, then they were gone.

"Good," scoffed Billy. "I didn't like having dumb wild animals in the house."

Buck started to speak, changed his mind and instead hugged Beth. "They're happier now," he said softly. "Tom and Jerry will raise families of their own, up on the mountain."

Buck watched closely, as he cut his tobacco and harvested the corn, but he never saw the familiar earless squirrels. Cold weather brought the hunting season.

"Don't go," pleaded Beth. "You might shoot Tom or Jerry. And I could *never* eat squirrel again."

"Don't worry,"chuckled Buck. "I'd recognize those two anywhere. They probably live across the mountain anyway. Besides, Beth, I've hunted all my life. It's my nature. A man's got to hunt."

He hunted, but found himself unable to enjoy stalking the squirrels, and he pulled back without shooting. "Danged pets," he said, smiling, "they got me to where I can't even shoot a strange squirrel. Beth, you've ruined it for me."

††††††

During the Thanksgiving vacation, while Buck, Annie, and Beth were gone shopping, two of Billy's friends came to visit. The boys eagerly eyed Buck's weapons.

"Do you go hunting, Billy?" asked one.

"Well," stalled Billy, "not very much."

"Let's go now."

Billy hesitated. "I don't know ..."

"Heck," scoffed one boy. "I bet you ain't allowed to shoot."

Billy stepped boldly forward and jerked down Buck's big shotgun. "I'll show you," he snapped. He stuffed green shells into his pocket. "Let's go."

The noisy, laughing trio, stopping to shoot at every target, gave ample warning as they climbed the mountain. All wild game vanished. After two hours of searching the boys grew weary, and started home. They left the mountain, walked across the cornfield, and one of the boys grabbed Billy's arm. "Look over yonder!" he screeched.

Atop a fence post, tail twisted, an adult gray squirrel perched, curious and unafraid. "Blast him, Billy!" The two boys danced eagerly. "Kill him!"

The squirrel waited, head cocked to listen. "Hurry up, Billy! Shoot him!"

Billy thumbed back the hammers and lifted the barrels. The squirrel watched.

Slowly, Billy pulled the trigger.

The shotgun bucked, and the squirrel flew raggedly from the post. "You got him!" The squirrel hit the ground, dragging, and scrambled away into the underbrush. "Come outa there!" shrieked the boys. They jammed sticks down the hole they found, pounded and yelled happily, finally gave up and walked excitedly on to the house.

Buck, puzzled, greeted them at the door. "Been target shootin?" he asked. "Sounded like a war, up on the mountain."

"Billy shot one, Mr. Hamilton," squealed one of the boys. "He got a squirrel, up in the cornfield!"

"You did?" Buck was uneasy. "Where is it?"

"It went down a hole," said Billy. "We couldn't get it out."

"Tom!" shrieked Beth. "You shot Tom!"

"Naw I didn't," said Billy. "This'n was a great big old gray squirrel. Not one of your old pets."

Beth was calm, the visitors were gone, and Buck sat quietly before the fireplace. Billy fidgeted. "*They* wanted to go," he blurted. "They said I couldn't shoot. It *was* a big old squirrel, daddy. Not Tom or Jerry."

"I believe you, son," sighed Buck. "But, next time you decide to go huntin, come with me. It ain't safe for a bunch of boys to go out with a shotgun playin. I'll teach you to hunt, if you want to learn."

"Yes, sir," said Billy. "Could I bring Larry and Chuck?"

Buck smiled forlornly. "Sure. I'll teach all three of you."

††††††

Only Buck was not asleep. He slumped before the fire, vaguely discontent, unhappy with the turn of events.

He and Annie had argued. "It's what you've always wanted," she had insisted. "Now that Billy finally wants to hunt, you go actin all silly."

"*He* don't want to hunt," said Buck. "It's them boys. Billy'll do whatever they tell 'im to do. It ain't the same, Annie."

"I declare, Buck," Annie had said angrily. "You are the strangest man."

††††††

Buck walked wearily to the kitchen, found the bourbon bottle under the sink, and splashed amber liquid into a water glass. He sipped, coughed, and sat the glass on the table. "Need more firewood," he grunted.

He opened the door and started outside, then froze. The screen was torn, clawed, shredded at the base. Buck eased the door open, and slumped to his knees.

Already stiff, bloody from buckshot, the dead squirrel lay at his feet. He rolled the body over with trembling hands. There were no ears, nothing sticking up.

The wounded squirrel had come home, and had died as it sought the protection of the cage.

Buck moaned, slammed the door, and walked out across the

yard. He leaned against a tree, trembling, pounding the bark in quiet frustration, gulping the cold night air. He clenched his teeth and started back inside, to wake Billy, then stopped at the steps.

"No," he mumbled. "Wouldn't do no good at all." He stared down at the stiff body for a long time, then took a deep breath and did what he had to do.

Buck bent, gently picked up the dead squirrel, carried it past the barn, dug a hole and carefully concealed the traces of the new grave. Stooped, tears streaming, he walked slowly back to the house. He gulped down the glass of bourbon, poured more, then carried the bottle with him, back to his chair by the fireplace.

"Man's got to hunt," he muttered softly. He stared into the glowing ashes. "He's got to."

SHIPPING OUT

He was stiff and self-conscious in the dress uniform, uneasy still with his role as new adult and soldier, awkwardly carrying the muscle and bulk added to his lean frame during basic training. The sudden intimacy of the uncles, their open acceptance into their private world, was distracting; and Arly was nervously aware of the admiring glances from the aunts and nieces.

Arly Rogers Boone, barely twenty, was a newcomer to manhood. In three short, frantic months he had acquired a crisp high school diploma, a letter of greetings from the draft board, and the solid, closecropped maturity of the US Army's Ft. Knox training camp. Arly was home on his first leave, two weeks before reporting to South Carolina and pre-Vietnam special camp. His voice was husky and crisp; his posture was ramrod correct and his every movement was precise, soldierly.

He finished eating, folded his napkin to a neat square, sat erect in the cornshuck bottomed chair, and surveyed the table he shared with his father, grandfather, and four uncles. Today Arly had not needed his mother's encouragement to wear the crisp uniform and glossy shoes, for every man at the table was a proud military veteran.

Zachariah Boone, the patriarch, sat at the head of the table. Zach was a WW I cavalry vet, one of the last of the daring branch; his long boots and saber were on display in the parlor. His four older sons fought WW II in Europe and the South Pacific, and Billy, the youngest, served in Korea with the Marines.

Two of the Boones had died in combat. Will, Zach's older brother, was buried in France, and Buck, the fifth son, had been killed in the opening hours of the Battle of the Bulge. The Boone men were openly proud of Arly, their newest soldier, the first of the current generation to serve the flag.

Arly's mother blushed with pride at every compliment, and hovered close to serve more chicken, biscuits, and cobbler. The younger children watched in quiet awe of their uniformed cousin, huddling close enough to listen. The grandmother, gray and barely eighty pounds, wiped her hands on her apron and regarded Arly with unabashed love and pleasure.

"Pauline," she told his mother, "Arly, he's the purtiest youngen you and Seth got."

Pauline smiled. "You always said that, Mamma Boone. I reckon he's been your favorite since you borned him."

†††††

The river had swirled and shoved, lapping at the timbers of the sunporch, cutting away at the ribbon slash of roadway, isolating Seth Boone's cabin on a temporary island of mud and rock. This would be Pauline's third baby in five years, and Dora knew her pattern. The birth would be soon, well before Seth could return with the doctor, and she readied the clean sheets.

Dora was right. The baby came in thirty minutes, a red and squalling and fat boy child, a shaggy haired and brown eyed Boone. Dora cleaned him, and laid him gently on his mother's warm belly. "Hit's a boy, Pauline," she said softly. "He'll be Arly, after my grandsir. Arly Rogers Boone."

"That's fine, Mamma Boone." Pauline was drowsy, exhausted. "Is Seth back yit?"

"Nope," said Dora. "The river's up bad, and I reckon the road is plumb gone."

It was near noon of the following day before Seth and the doctor arrived, muddy and tired from the struggle. They found

Dora rocking the new baby before a crackling fireplace, and she opened the blanket to show them. "Ain't he the purtiest thing?" she asked.

†††††

"Grandma," said Arly, "come out and look at my new car." He stood a foot taller, and he cuddled her gently in one strong arm.

"I'd be proud to," said Dora.

Arly's farm savings and first Army pay had made the down payment on the sparkling new 1965 Chevrolet Impala convertible, white with red seats and shining wheel covers. Dora inspected the car carefully. "Law, Arly, hit's somethin," she said. "But ain't it got no roof?"

He laughed. "It's a convertible, grandma. The top comes up when you push that button there."

"I do declare," said Dora. "Hit's a mighty fine car, Arly."

He grinned happily, and wiped away the road dust from the mirror.

Dora patted the red seatback. "Hit shore is lots finer than what we rode ye in the first time. Do ye remember, Arly? When we rode ye to Newport fer yer first shoes? And picture? And we got ye the haircut?"

"No, grandma," smiled Arly. "I don't remember."

†††††

Seth was in Detroit, building cars, the day Arly turned two.

Chubby, blonde curls to his shoulders, Arly was his grandmother's delight, her favorite of the offspring and her constant companion. She determined to have his portrait made, to buy him hard soled shoes, and to make a visit to the barber. She enlisted Pauline for the excursion, and took wrinkled bills and dull silver from a leather pouch.

The women harnessed the mules, hitched them to the green Studebaker wagon, and left Boone Mountain at daybreak. Arly and his two sisters slept under homemade quilts as the wagon crossed Cox Gap and rattled beside the creek, Dora sawing at the reins and Pauline working the brake lever. In Newport Dora parked the wagon by the courthouse, tied the lead rein to a parking meter, and ignored the stares as she led her small brood on the mission.

The barber charged ten cents, and saved the curls. The photographer, for two dollars, promised delivery of two five by seven tinted photographs. The shoes were stiff, white, ankle high, ugly and uncomfortable. Arly wept, whimpered, took the barber's stick of striped candy, and refused to wear the shoes. The ride home took hours, and the moon was high when the lanterns led the wagon home to the Boone cabin.

The portraits arrived a month later. Dora's still hung over the living room mantle, joined only today by Arly's official Army 8 X 10 in a gilded frame.

††††††

Arly's Aunt Charlotte, only two years older, joined them by the new convertible. "Give us a ride, soldier?" Her ready smile flashed.

"Law, not me," protested Dora. "You youngens go on."

Arly turned the Chevy carefully, and drove slowly on the gravel road, trailed by a swirl of dust. On the paved highway he picked up speed, and the warm wind whipped at Charlotte's long black hair and billowed her dress around slim brown legs. She smiled, slid across the seat, snuggled close, and Arly breathed the familiar perfume. He slipped his arm around her shoulders and pulled her closer in a fierce hug.

"Remember?" she asked softly.

"How could I ever forget?" answered Arly.

††††††

She had been fourteen; Arly was twelve.

Together they had climbed the mountain, and lay panting on a grassy slope, barefooted, fingers loosely touching, watching the clouds scoot past overhead. Below, at the Boone homeplace, the aunts and uncles and cousins were gathered for the July 4 reunion, dripping cold watermelon and homemade ice cream, spilling out from the long covered porch to fill the shaded yard and to clutter the woodlot. Children splashed in the creek, men huddled over furtive flasks, and the women busily restocked the long tables and ran back and forth to the steamy kitchen. From the mountain it was a busy anthill, and Charlotte giggled as she watched. She sat erect, her dress gathered around her hips, dusty and skinny and intense.

"Watch 'em, Arly," she sniffed. "Feedin ·their faces." She made a wry face of her own. "All they want to do is eat, then eat some more."

"Yeah," Arly agreed lazily. "But what'd you druther do?"

"Oh." Charlotte shrugged. "See a movie show. Go to Ashland. Fly in an airplane. Be a movie star."

Arly chuckled.

"Or," Charlotte added, "make love."

"What?" Arly jerked around. "Do you even know how?"

She scowled. "Of course I do, dummy."

"Have you . .?"

"Well, no," she said primly. "I ain't ever actually *done it* yit, but I'm goin to."

"I'll bet," grinned Arly.

"I am," laughed Charlotte. "Right now, with you." She giggled and lept quickly, tumbling Arly and pinning his shoulders. She leaned forward and kissed his dry lips. "Don't you want to?"

Arly stared, gulped, then smiled slowly. "Yeah," he mumbled. "I want to."

"You ain't mad at me, are you?" asked Charlotte.

"Naw." He turned. "I jist . . we . . ."

"Arly Boone!" Charlotte stamped her foot and glared. "You are the dumbest thing." She grabbed his arm, and looked up at him. Their eyes locked. "We can't do it. We're cousins."

Arly finally relaxed, and grinned. "Yeh. We are, ain't we?"

"What's the matter with you?" Charlotte stared.

He laughed. "Let's git back down yonder. I'm so hungry I could eat a horse."

††††††

"You'd better get me back to the house," giggled Charlotte. "Before we get in trouble."

As they made the turn back toward the Boone homeplace she squeezed his hand fiercely. "Goodbye, Arly," she whispered. "You take care of yourself, and come back here as soon as you can." Charlotte slid across the seat as they neared the crowd, and joined her husband and baby on the porch. Arly watched, smiling wistfully, then walked on alone past the house. He wound through the woodlot, close by the henhouse, then followed the cornfield toward the barn.

The corn was tall, turning brown, heavy with yellow ears. On the hillside above were haystacks, pointed straw igloos, winter food for the livestock. Zach's grayed mules grazed sleepily near the water trough, switching at the occasional fly and peering somberly at the solitary walker. In the barn driveway Arly could see the yellow spokes of the wagon wheels, tall under the green sideboards and red leafspring seat, and two sets of worn harness hung on wooden pegs.

He walked on, daydreaming and remembering, ambling slowly past the barn and down the narrow roadway to the creek. He stopped, abrupt and suddenly alert; he chilled, listening to the solid stillness, searching quickly for the danger, for the reason the birds were quiet. He found it, and his breath hissed out slowly. A fat, three foot copperhead was stretched across the roadway, five feet ahead, lethal and silent and ominous.

Arly backed away, treading carefully, every sense tingling.

††††††

He had blushed proudly as Dora bragged, looked down at his feet and grinned as she told the story to his uncles.

"Arly, he's got a extry sense," she swore. "That boy, he can tell when hit's dangerous, tell without seein.'' He squirmed and tugged his cap lower. "He jist knowed it was out there," beamed Dora. "He never seen that snake, but he knowed it was there and he come a runnin to git me away."

Arly had been fifteen, spending his last full summer on Boone Mountain. Later he discovered baseball and girls and cars and other distractions which led him different ways, and this final summer as a child he'd stayed close to Dora. Somehow they both knew the summer was the last; both sensed the impending separation.

Arly had dragged Dora out from the corn, deposited her safely by the barn, and run back with the sharp hoe. He posed bashfully for the picture, the copperhead stretched at his feet, one arm around his tiny grandmother and the other lifted in a triumphant salute.

††††††

His eyes focused again on the immediate danger, and he looked for a weapon. He found the heavy rock, lifted it, and stopped. There was no use in killing the snake; no one else was close. Arly hesitated, remembered the smaller children playing at the cabin, and grimly attacked.

He walked back, joined his father and uncles behind the smokehouse, squatted with them as they passed the quart bottle. He listened politely until there was a break, and offered his comment. "Had to kill a copperhead," he grunted. "Big one, almost four feet. It was down by the barn."

"They thick this summer," frowned Seth. "It's a gittin to where I'm skeered fer the littleuns to play out away from the house." He drank, wiped the lip of the jar, and passed it to Arly. "Better git used to this stuff," he advised, grinning. "It'll make them damn sergeants look a hell of a lot more like humans."

"Even if they ain't," chuckled Wesley. "Lord, Arly, I outlived many a damn officer." He took the bottle and sipped. "We said we was winnin the last war, back in '45. The war to end 'em all." He laughed sourly. "Then Billy, he went off to Korea, and now you're headed fer China."

"Vietnam," corrected Arly.

"Same difference," said Wesley. "We ain't a tryin to win."

"I hear them women over there is somethin else," grinned Alvin. "Jist don't you ketch no diseases can't be cured."

Arly smiled. "Did you, Uncle Alvin?"

"None that they couldn't cure with a shot," said Alvin.

They chuckled, and the jar passed around.

"You watch out fer yerself over there, boy," Earl said seriously. "Don't you volunteer fer nothin, and if they start a shootin git in behind some big feller."

Arly laughed.

"Don't laugh, damnit," growled Earl. "Buck, he never listened, and . . ." His voice trailed away to an uneasy silence.

"Better give me another pull at that jar," said Arly. "I need the blood thinner."

The forced smiles made everyone uneasy, and the group drifted away, each man to his own thoughts.

†††††

They were gone, Seth and Pauline and the others, but Arly

lingered. Finally, reluctantly, he walked to the convertible.

Dora stopped him. "Let yer old grandma git a good look at ye, Arly, afore ye go." She stood before him, gazing up. "My, my," she sighed. "You are a sight, Arly."

He bent, blushing and blinking back the tears, to clasp both her wrinkled hands. "I'll be here for Christmas next year," he promised. "Won't seem like any time at all. You'll see, **Grandma.**"

He hugged her quickly, lifting her off the ground, then stumbled to the car, fumbling for the ignition through wet eyes, and finally started the engine.

"Watch out fer yerself," yelled Earl.

Arly smiled stiffly, swung the Chevy in a tight circle, snapped a jaunty salute to the uncles, and gunned the car forward. In the rear view mirror he watched; Charlotte moved quickly to hug Dora, and Uncle Earl stared wistfully after him.

††††††

At the crest of Boone Gap was the family graveyard, final resting place for six generations, and here Arly parked. He climbed the barb wire fence, searched, and found his Uncle Buck's marker.

Buck (Vernon Albert Boone, the marker said) had been almost eighteen, eager to join his older brothers, afraid the fighting would end before he was old enough. He had cajoled **Dora into signing the enlistment papers, four months before he** died in the smoking machine gun pit in France.

His brothers, stern and fierce in full dress uniforms, had been sent home to carry young Buck to the mountain.

††††††

He grew up right here, thought Arly. Same hills, same people, same games and playing places. Buck must have laughed and sung and loved, learned about life in this very place, and left proud in his new uniform to serve his country. Young Buck Boone would have left cocky, laughed and told his mother not to worry, walked away with his head high to conceal the terror, his shoulders square as he marched toward victory.

††††††

The fear swept Arly; he slumped to the barren grave and wept for his young uncle and for himself.

THE LIBERATION OF ELSIE WATTS

Elsie Anette was the oldest of Eva and Mack Ward's fourteen offspring.

At six Elsie was doing the family wash, beating the clothes clean on the rocks of Caney Creek, pressing out the wrinkles with irons heated over the big cookstove. At eleven she quit school to help at home, cooking and cleaning and caring for the new babies.

Mack Ward held 400 acres of rugged Eastern Kentucky hillside farm land, and he bred new workers at the rate of one per summer. Eva, willing but weary, was unable to do more than bear the babies, and young Elsie became the surrogate mother. She was caretaker for the busy household, cook and comforter to the other children, expert at quilting and sewing, soap-making and canning and cooking.

At thirteen Elsie was prime marriage material, strong and pretty and blossoming, skilled and proven reliable. The first suitors showed up as soon as Mack would permit their visits. They were rawboned young farmers, awkward in starched work clothes, hair slicked with possum fat, rough hands nervously busy rolling Bull Durham. The more wealthy rode up on prancing saddle mares with braided manes and jingling silver bridles, and others hitched their somber mules at the barn and walked the last half mile.

Saturday night meant banjos and fiddles and guitars, and a crowd gathered around Mack's big battery powered Philco radio. There was moonshine and bootleg whiskey, singing and fistfighting, preening for Elsie and serious responsibility to impress Mack.

Elsie was curious, but disinterested, until Harper Watts made his first visit. Harper was 22, strutting, flashing a wide smile, blessed with curly black hair and dancing eyes. Two days before Elsie's fifteenth birthday they were married, and a week later Elsie was expecting. The first daughter was born, then a son, and Elsie was pregnant again when Pearl Harbor was bombed. Harper enlisted, left for four years in the South Pacific, and Elsie endured.

The second son was born while Harper was gone, and Elsie was expecting another a month after the soldier came home. Harper, after seeing New York and San Francisco, was unable to adjust again to Sparks Ridge. He took his growing family west, closer to the edge of the mountains, to a tenant farm near the Kentucky River. Harper farmed, labored on a bridge crew, tinkered with cars and worked as a carpenter, struggled to earn a meager existence for his brood. Elsie bore two more babies, then twins, and finally the last, a son born when she was 33.

It was Elsie's task to stretch the budget. She worked a two acre garden, tended a flock of leghorn chickens, raised hogs to butcher on Thanksgiving, canned beans and blackberries and tomatoes, dressed and cooked the game Harper brought in with his .22 rifle. She sewed the girls' dresses and the boys' shirts, doctored the cuts and bruises and fevers, soothed the adolescent frustrations, and sent the little Watts off to school scrubbed and with full bellies.

For four decades Elsie labored, guiding her flock through first loves and graduations and weddings, babies and brawls and heartbreaks, always available to provide comfort and strength. Harper's hot supper was ready every day at four-thirty, his lunchbox was packed each morning before dawn, and she brought the pipe and coffee when he rested.

Harper, as the children left home, was able to finally rest. He cut back to one full time job, bought a used color TV, and found time again to sip the good Sparks Ridge moonshine. His worn easy chair was a throne, from where Harper presided over the weekend gatherings of his clan. For Harper Watts, the hard part was over.

Elsie was less fortunate.

She served as free babysitter to two dozen grandchildren, chef and dishwasher for the Sunday reunions, advisor and curtain maker to nine households, servant to Harper's whims, and overseer of the small farm. When Bub, the youngest, enlisted in the Army, Elsie was also stranded, isolated and totally dependant on Harper for any transportation.

Alone—for the first time in her life—Elsie brooded. Uneducated, unsophisticated, unskilled at any profession, Elsie fretted and grieved. She was over fifty, taken for granted, restless now with her enforced housewifery.

On her 54th birthday Elsie was up at five to bake her own cake and serve dinner to 37 children and grandchildren, and was elbow deep in soapy dishwater when she made her decision.

Dripping, twisting her apron, redfaced and determined, Elsie descended upon the living room assembly.

"Harper Watts!" she screeched, "I've had enough of this!" She wheeled and was gone.

Harper, slackjawed and stunned, stared after Elsie until his cigarette burned down to his finger. He swore, jerked, and kicked over the table full of ashtrays and coffee cups. Plaintively, he turned to face his sons and daughters.

"What do you all reckon," he asked feebly, "has got into your mommy?"

††††††

At first Harper was quietly proud of Elsie.

"For a woman she's comin right along," he told a friend. "Bub, he's teachin her how to drive, and she's takin the test next week. It ain't like Elsie *needs* a drivin license, you know. I take her anywhere's she needs to go, and now we got one of them telephones."

Bub, home on a 30 day leave, tried to prepare Harper.

"She's looking for a job, daddy," he said warily.

Harper chuckled. "Who'd hire her? Your mamma ain't ever done nothin but clean house and change diapers."

"I'm just telling you," persisted Bub. "Mamma is serious. She'll find work, somewhere."

Harper grinned. "That'll be the day, Bub."

Elsie passed the driving test, and Harper selected and paid for the old Vega station wagon. "Keeps her happy," he told the children. "Gotta humor mountain women."

Elsie's first solo trip, to town on Saturday for groceries, went well until she started home. She reached to steady a sack of corn meal, and looked up just as the Vega left the pavement and flew across a deep ditch. Elsie flattened four fence posts, clipped the legs out from under a water tank, hit a corncrib and rolled, landing upside down in a muddy pen of squalling piglets. She crawled out the window, slipped and fell in the muck, crawled to the fence to escape the angry sow, and wailed as she watched her shattered car sink deeper.

After ten minutes Elsie wiped her nose, shooed away the confused brood sow, salvaged her groceries, and walked stiffly home.

Harper, an hour later, found the wreckage. He searched frantically, swearing, and drove home in a panic. He found Elsie, calmly dishing out supper, expressionless. "You're late," she snapped. "And go wipe the mud off your feet."

"But . . . I . . . you . . ." Harper's temper flared and he sputtered; he reconsidered after a look at Elsie's face and washed up for the meal. Elsie broke the silence. "I reckon you seen it?"

"Your car?" Harper's lip twitched. "Is it the one layin up yonder in Willie's hog lot?"

"You and the boys'll have to git it out, and fix Willie's fence and stuff." Elsie chewed solemnly.

"I reckon we will," grunted Harper. He grinned. "Kill any pigs?"

"No!" snapped Elsie.

After supper they sat beside the fireplace. "Harper," Elsie finally said, "I ain't gonna quit drivin."

"I don't know about that," scowled Harper. " 'Pears to me you orta give it up, Elsie. Besides, you ain't got nothin to drive."

"I do too," said Elsie. "Albert already found me a Buick."

"You bought a car?"

"Yes."

"But . . you never asked me."

"No." Elsie smiled. "I never, did I?" She left him staring and went off to bed.

††††††

The hospital administrator chuckled as Elsie left, and called for his assistant. "Do you know that woman who was just here?" he asked.

"No."

"She's 54 years old, went to school for less than five years, has never had a job, and I just hired her."

"As a maid?"

"Nope." He laughed. "Elsie Watts is our new recreation director for the extended care wing."

"Have you lost your mind?"

"Maybe. But, Maggie, that woman has raised nine children, and run a household since she was six. Can you think of any better preparation for taking care of twenty old people?"

"Can Mrs. Watts read and write?"

"Not like you and me, but she can sure get a message across."

††††††

"You done what?" Harper's fork stopped in mid air.

"I told you," said Elsie. "I got a job. At the hospital."

Harper puzzled. "Cookin?"

Elsie glared. "No, I'll be takin care of the older people. Gittin 'em haircuts, and games, and preachers for Sunday, and stuff like that."

Harper grunted. "I'll be danged."

"Is that all you got to say?" asked Elsie.

"I reckon so." Harper finished eating and sat quietly.

Elsie spent her first day on the job watching, meeting the other workers and the patients, and did not get home until after six. Harper met her at the door. "Where in the Hell is supper?" he growled.

"You can just wait 'till I git it cooked," Elsie said calmly, "or fix it yourself, or do without." She marched past him to change clothes, then warmed up Sunday's chicken and dumplings.

"This ain't gonna work," grumbled Harper. "I durn near starved to death."

Elsie studied the hospital manuals until eleven, then slept in the spare bedroom.

††††††

Elsie's first challenge came during her third week on the job.

Sadie Weaver, 86 years old and a terminal cancer patient, disrupted the floor by angrily accusing the head nurse of stealing her baby. Persistent, tearful, heartbroken, the old woman struggled and wailed and was finally sedated. Elsie grieved.

"It ain't right," she told the nurse. "We can't jist let her lay there and cry like that."

"What would *you* do?" snapped the nurse. "Get her a baby?"

"Maybe," said Elsie. "Maybe I would, at that."

The next morning Elsie was early, and she carried a small

bundle to Sadie's room.

"Praise God," cried Sadie. "My prayers is answered, El-sie." She hugged the worn doll close to withered breasts. "I knowed," she said, "that my baby was here somewheres. That woman stoled it, Elsie, and you brung it back."

Elsie blinked back her tears and left quickly.

All day, Sadie proudly showed her baby to everyone in the hospital, and even Eb Weaver gently cuddled the doll when he came to visit. The indignant nurse went straight to the admini-strator. "That woman," she sputtered, "Elsie Watts actually gave Sadie Weaver a *doll*! Mr. Smith, I've had it. I've never seen anything so outrageous. I insist that you fire Elsie Watts im-mediately."

The administrator rocked back in his chair, and smiled. "How has Sadie Weaver been today?"

"She's been too busy holding that doll," snapped the nurse, "to do anything else."

"She didn't cause any trouble?"

"No."

"Seems to me," he said quietly, "that Elsie did us all a big favor."

"Well . . . in a way . . . I guess . . ." The nurse reddened. "Maybe she did, but she violated all routine and procedure and—"

"Miss Barton," the administrator said, "Elsie Watts gave a dying woman a day of happiness. Isn't that what we're sup-posed to do?"

After the angry nurse was gone the administrator called down to the personnel office. "Elsie Watts is now a permanent employee," he ordered. He smiled. "She just passed all the tests."

††††††

Harper Watts mourned.

Elsie's suppers were late, even cold, and she often went back to town for evening programs. Once, for an entire weekend, Elsie was in Louisville for a workshop—her first night ever away from home, Harper's first night alone. Elsie spent her paycheck as she pleased, without consulting Harper, and on Sunday afternoons she drove to visit her family on Sparks Ridge and to church services.

"It ain't natural," Harper complained to Priscilla, the oldest daughter. "Your mommy is out runnin all the time, and spendin money like she was rich. She told me she ain't got time to cook our Sunday dinners nomore, either." He shook his head. "I don't know what's come over her, Prissy."

"*I* work," said Priscilla. "Lots of women do, daddy. You'll get used to it."

The tension built. Harper compounded the problem by bringing home a dog, a wolfish German Shepherd considered hopeless by its previous owners.

"You'll be sorry," warned Elsie. "That thing'll kill one of the little ones, and then what'll you do?"

Harper stubbornly ignored her, kept the dog, and three weeks later Buck did nip a grandchild who ventured too near the food dish.

"That thing has got to go," said Elsie. "Take him to the woods and shoot him."

"Buck, he's *my* dog," said Harper. "Besides, he never hurt the boy none."

Elsie stormed off to the bedroom.

Even Harper found it difficult to like the clumsy and surly animal, and made only half hearted attempts to train him. Buck, a drooling 125 pound dullard, forced the issue. First he killed six of Elsie's hens, then left a mauled kitten on the front steps. Elsie paled, slipped angrily back into the house, and came out lugging Harper's old double barreled shotgun.

"Come here, Buck," she chirped.

Buck thundered around the corner, skidded and backpedaled,

and howled as Elsie's first load of buckshot peppered his flanks. Her second charge spattered around him as he ran, whimpering, for the safety of the barn.

Harper came home, found his subdued and trembling dog, packed his straight razor and shirts, loaded Buck into the pickup and drove to Priscilla's to stay.

"I left her," he explained angrily. "A man can't live with no woman what'd shoot his dog."

†††††

After a week of Harper and Buck, Priscilla convened a council of the Watts offspring. "You've got to help me," she pleaded. "Daddy's too stubborn to go back, and mommy's feelings are hurt so bad she won't apologize. And *I'm* about ready to shoot that dog again."

It was Bub, preoccupied as he drove in from Ft. Knox, who unintentionally triggered the solution. He lost control on the wet highway, slid into a tree and flipped, rolled out of the car and lay unconscious.

†††††

Elsie took the call from the state police, and arrived at the hospital minutes behind the ambulance, just ahead of Harper and Priscilla.

"They don't know yet," choked Elsie. "Bub's in there with the doctors." She spoke only to Priscilla. "You tell your daddy."

"I heard," grunted Harper. "Prissy, ask your mommy did she see Bub when they brung him in?"

Priscilla sighed. "Did you, mamma?"

"For a second," sobbed Elsie. "He was all wet, and still." She dissolved into tears and clung to Priscilla. Harper fidgeted, dark and gloomy, big hands flexing.

They waited, awkward and anxious, for the half hour before the door opened. "Bub's fine," the doctor said quickly. "Cut and bruised, but more scared than anything. We'll keep him overnight to be sure, but there's nothing to worry about. I gave him a sedative, so he's sleeping now. It'll be a while before he can talk."

"Thankee, doc," Harper said gravely.

"That's why I'm here," said the doctor. "That goes for all of us here at the hospital, including Elsie." He smiled. "I've been meaning to tell you, Harper, what a fine job Elsie does for us. You can be proud of her."

"I am." Harper studied his toes, and Elsie stared down the hallway.

Priscilla found her raincoat. "I'd better go," she said. "I'll tell everybody Bub's okay. Mamma, you bring daddy home."

"Jist a minute now," blurted Harper. "I'll ride with you, Prissy."

"No you won't," said Elsie. "You'll stay right here. That's your baby layin in there. You can come back for him later, Priscilla."

Priscilla folded. "Okay," she said wearily. "Call me when you're ready, daddy. I'll send somebody for you."

Elsie and Harper waited at opposite ends of the room until a nurse called them. Bub grinned feebly as they entered. "I guess I'll have to quit making fun of your driving, mamma." Elsie squeezed his hand and gently stroked his forehead. "How's my car?" asked Bub.

"Don't you go worryin about no car," said Elsie.

"Was you drinkin, boy?" asked Harper. His face was stern.

"Harper!" Elsie spun, spitting. "You stop it!"

Bub groaned. "*You* stop it, mamma. I'm not up to any more of the two of you fighting."

"Fightin?" Elsie stared. "Why, we ain't . . ." She blushed, and looked down at the floor. "I guess we was," she said quietly.

Bub chuckled. "You sure were. Like two old settin hens. That's why I was on my way home. We were all going to talk it over and see what we could do."

"We?" asked Harper. "Is that why they was all out to Prissy's?"

"Yeah," said Bub. "She called me, all worried about you two."

"Dang it," started Harper, "You all ain't got no business meddlin in—"

"Shut up, Harper," Elsie said softly. "We can talk somewheres else."

They stayed for an hour, and left Bub sleeping soundly.

†††††††

Elsie buttoned her coat and waited at the lobby door. "Harper," she said. "I'm sorry I shot old Buck. Did I hurt him bad?"

Harper shuffled closer. "Naw," he muttered, "to tell you the truth, he's been doin lots better since you peppered him." His brown eyes sparkled. "Elsie, I been missin you."

"Me too." Elsie frowned. "Harper, are you comin home?"

He took a wary step backwards. "I'm wantin to," he said. "Are you gonna keep on workin?"

"Yes." Her answer was firm and quick. "That's the way it's got to be, Harper."

He grinned, and shrugged. "Can't blame a man for tryin, can you?" He stepped closer and gently touched Elsie's shoulder. "I'll come home if you'll have me, Elsie."

"I ain't never wanted nobody else," said Elsie. "Not since the day I first seen you."

Harper coughed and shuffled nervously. "Let's go home."

"You drive," said Elsie.

"Nope," said Harper. "It's high time I seen for myself how you handle a car."

In the parking lot Elsie nervously started the old Buick,

edged backwards, shifted gears and gunned the engine, and slammed hard into a light pole.

She screamed.

Harper pulled himself up from the floorboard, rubbed his chin, adjusted his cap, and finally grinned.

"Try her again, Elsie," he grunted. "I believe they's a pole over yonder that you missed."

PATTON

"Ovey, I brung you a present."

Ezry Hall pushed back his cap to show a balding forehead, opened the truck door and climbed out. He reached back in and brought out a rat-wire cage, suitcase size, with a long handle. He held, high and an arm's length away, swung it over and sat it on the stump.

"C'mere, youngens. Lookit this."

Jody, Suse, Ovey, and Annie gathered shyly, and the black hound Buck barked frantically, trying to pull Jody away.

"Git, Buck!" snapped Ezry. "Tie the durn fool up, Jody."

Jody dragged Buck away and snapped the chain, then ran back.

The bottom of the cage was lined with straw, and there was movement.

"Stay back, youngens," warned Ezry. He twisted a limb from the maple tree and gently prodded the cage.

The straw exploded.

The flimsy cage rattled, bits of hay flew wildly, and the buzzing started. Up from the bedding, swaying, tongue flickering, reared a fanged and darting head.

Suse screamed and ran. Ovey dived for Ezry's legs, and Annie fainted. Jody had the chopping axe in mid-air when Ezry caught him.

"Dangnation!" yelled Ezry. "Ain't none of you never seen no rattlesnake afore?"

The buzzing was louder, faster, and Buck howled, lunging against his chain. Ezry wiggled the branch and the rattler struck, slamming against the wire and chewing. Annie stumbled to her feet and ran, squalling, for the shelter of the cabin. Ezry picked Ovey loose from his leg.

"Dang it," he said wearily, "It's a pet. He can't git loose."

Jody edged closer. 'Godamighty," he said in awe. "Where'd you git 'im, Pap?"

Ezry grinned proudly. "Down to the store. Jeb Stone, he give him to me fer three dollar, cage and all. Caught him up on Turtle Mountain, he said."

"What are we gonna do with him?" asked Jody.

"I told you, he's a pet." Ezry was exasperated. "We gonna keep him, and feed him, and take keer of him."

"Why?" asked Jody, backing away, still holding the axe.

"Dadgumit!" snapped Ezry. "You youngens got cats 'n dogs 'n chickens 'n pigs runnin all over. I done got me a pet, by durn."

Ovey circled the cage, fascinated. He reached out and the rattler struck. Ovey laughed, eyes sparkling.

"Jeb said to give him live mice and rats and stuff. And milk. He dranks right smart milk, Jeb said, and sometimes a aig."

Ovey moved, and the rattler swayed to follow him.

"What's his name?"

"Jeb, he called him King," said Ezry. "But I'm thinkin he'd be Patton. After my gin'ril, in the war."

"Yeah," grinned Ovey. "That's good. It a boy er a girl?"

"Why, a boy, I reckon" Ezry scratched his head. "Can't say as I know how ye'd tell, though."

Ezry puzzled, then shrugged his shoulders. "Shut up yer hound, Jody," he ordered, "and Ovey, you go git us some milk and we'll feed old Patton here."

Jody sat with Buck, and consoled the trembling hound. "He ain't nothin but a big old snake, Buck. Iffen I let ye go he'd sure kill you. He ain't no blacksnake, Buck." The hound whined, licked Jody's hand, and watched closely as Ovey ran from the cabin carrying a Mason jar lid filled with milk.

"How we gonna git it in there, Pap?"

"I dunno, Ovey." Ezry took off his cap and ran his hand through the thin hair. "Jeb, he never tol me that." He studied the cage. "They's a little door, over here." He frowned. "Maybe we can hold 'im with a stick and slip the milk in real fast."

He moved closer to the cage, and the rattlers sung. "Fierce old feller, ain't he?" He chuckled. "Jis like a old boar hog."

Ezry flipped open his Barlow and used the blade to jiggle open the cage door. Patton backed away, head high, rattles singing.

"He's might like a goose," said Ezry, "so busy tryin to skeer everbody he'll fergit to bite."

He raised the door. "I can't set this in there, though," he said. "He'd git me fer sure . . . gimme that old can, Ovey."

He poured the milk into the rusty oil can. "Now watch," he grunted. He dropped the jar lid into the cage.

Patton struck, quickly, shaking the wire, and Ezry jumped back.

"See," he said, pointing to the overturned lid. "Now I kin jis pour the milk down from the top." He did, and they sat and waited.

Patton buzzed softly.

"How does snakes drank, Pap?" asked Ovey.

"Dang if I know," said Ezry. They watched together, squatted on their haunches.

"Ezry Hall what are you a doin bringin in a big ol snake to skeer my youngens half to death and—."

Berthy Hall's screeching stopped abruptly; she stared at Patton's blurring tail.

"Oh, God!" she screamed. "Oh my God he's brung a big ol rattlesnake! Run, youngens! Annie, git me the axe! Jody, git away from there! Ovey, Lord Ovey don't move!"

She ran, apron flapping, for the cabin. She came back dragging Ezry's old doublebarreled shotgun, jamming shells into the chambers as she ran.

"Git back!" she yelled, swinging the gun to her shoulder. She jerked both triggers. Ovey dived for the woodpile, and Ezry sprawled under the truck. The recoil sent Berthy backwards, head over heels into the rosebush.

The double charge of hot buckshot slammed into the stump, showering sawdust, lifting the cage. It toppled, and Patton buzzed wildly. Buck howled and lunged, broke the chain, and dragged Jody across the yard. The chickenhouse erupted in a cackling terror. Annie and Suse ran screaming, and Berthy's legs thrashed wildly among the thorns of the rosebush.

The dust settled.

Ezry peered out from behind the tire, and Ovey peeked over the stacked wood. Jody desperately hung to Buck, holding him as he growled and snapped.

Berthy broke free from the briars, redfaced and tight lipped, ripped her skirts loose and marched off to the cabin.

"Berthy June," yelled Ezry, "You come back here! You dang near kilt me and Ovey."

"Pap," screeched Ovey, "Patton, he's about to git loose."

Ezry turned his attention to the cage, ignoring the slamming cabin door, and leaped to push the cage upright and snap the latch.

The rattler gradually calmed, and quietened.

Suse tugged at Ezry's leg. "Here's yer gun Pap," she said solemnly. "Mam done dropped it right in the dirt." She pulled at the shotgun by its smoking barrels. "Did Mam kill yore new pet?"

"No she never, honey," said Ezry. "Your Mam, she was skeered, was all. She didn't mean to hurt nobody."

"She don't like yore snake, Pap." Suse was serious and intent. "But you let me keep all the kittens, so you kin have your pet too." She skipped away.

Ezry wiped his forehead.

"Help me git Buck tied back up," called Jody. "He's still a tryin to git at that old snake."

Ezry helped chain the dog, and they walked back to the cage. Ovey was hunkered close, smiling. "Pap," he said, "Patton, he's the bestest pet I ever seen. Kin he be mine too?"

"Reckon so," muttered Ezry. "You and me, we the onliest ones likes 'im. Let's put him in the shed."

Ezry carried the cage, Ovey close behind, to the corncrib. They sat the cage on a barrel, near a window. "The sun'll hit 'im here," said Ezry. "Snakes, they need lotsa sun."

"I'll ketch some mice," said Ovey, "and feed him."

"Wait till mornin," said Ezry. "We best get to supper fore it's cold."

"Is Mam mad? Is she gonna let us keep Patton?" Ovey was worried.

"I dunno," Ezry said softly, "she's mighty afeered of snakes. I don't know, Ovey."

They walked together, slowly, up the path.

The old cabin, set among the roses, was weathered and gray, home to seven generations of Halls since it was first built. It was a double sized cabin, two floors, with a porch running the width of the front. Fieldstones made the foundation, and steps led to each door. A giant fireplace stood at either end.

Inside the walls had been covered and papered, and a pot-bellied stove was in the center of the living room. The kitchen, where Berthy cooked over the woodstove, was large and cluttered with skillets, pans, and dried fruit hanging on the walls.

A long trestle table was set, and all but Ezry and Ovey were seated at their plates.

They joined the family, and they ate without speaking. The children nervously eyed both parents, but neither looked up.

Ovey broke the silence. "Mam, kin we keep Patton?"

"Keep who?" Berthy's fork stopped in midair.

"Patton. Mine and Pap's snake."

"*Yourn* and Pap's? I thought it was hissen."

"He done give me half."

Berthy stared coldly at Ezry, who suddenly was interested in the bent tine of his fork.

Ovey wept. "Jody, he's got Buck, and Suse has got all them cats, and Annie's got the rabbits—I ain't got nothin." He ran from the table.

Suse and Annie quietly followed.

"Ezry Hall," said Berthy. "You have done gone plumb crazy. Givin a baby a big old rattlesnake." She stood and angrily scraped the dishes. "A rattlesnake. Fer God's sake, Ezry!" She piled dishes in the washpan. Jody was watching. "Go git some water, Jody," she snapped.

Ezry rolled a cigarette, lit the damp paper, and shoved back his chair.

"Berthy June," he finally said, "That snake, he can't git loose. He ain't one whit a meaner'n your goose, and he don't make no noise. We're keepin him, me and Ovey, so's you jist better git used to the idea."

Jody returned with the water. "Ovey's down at the barn bawlin," he said.

Berthy relented. "OK. But don't bring it near my house. If it gits loose I'll kill it. And keep my babies away from it."

Ezry stood, grinning. "Shucks, Berthy, you couldn't kill him. He'd be plum to Hazard afore ye could hit him."

He ducked and ran, and the plate smashed against the door behind him.

"Bring Buck," Ezry told Jody, once he was safely out of throwing range. "Him and Patton's got to git friendly fore they kill each other."

"Nossir," swore Jody. "Buck, he ain't gonna make friends with no rattlesnake. He'd kill that old Patton with one bite."

"Jist bring 'im," ordered Ezry.

Buck pulled at his chain, sniffing and whining, hair bristled.

"Whoa, Buck," yelled Jody. "You ain't sposed to kill thisun. Hit's Pap's and Ovey's. Hit's a pet, Buck."

The hound's answer was a low, rumbling growl.

In the shed Ezry took Buck's chain and led him closer. Patton reared, buzzing, swaying. Buck sniffed, whined, and then raised a leg and wet on the barrel. He squatted, tongue out, and contemplated Patton. The rattling stopped.

"Good ol Buck," praised Jody.

"Patton'd kill 'im iffen he was loose," threatened Ovey, his face tearstained and his voice trembling.

"He couldn't neither," said Jody. "Let 'im out and I'll show you."

"None o' that," warned Ezry. "That snake stays in the cage, all of the time. You hear me, Ovey?"

"Yeah, Pap." Ovey hung his head. "But he could shore whup any old dog."

††††††

The care, feeding, and showing of Patton kept Ovey busy. He trapped mice and dropped them in the cage, brought milk every day, and even stole an egg from the henhouse. He never saw Patton eat, but the food vanished.

He was sure Patton knew him.

"He don't buzz at me," he bragged, "and he gits mad if anybody else comes in."

Ovey and the rattler were pictured in the county newspaper, with Buck close by. Neighbors came every day to marvel at the fangs and long row of rattles, and to praise Ovey for his bravery in caring for Patton.

"He's tamed now," said Ovey. "He knows the whole family, and he don't rattle at none of us ner at Buck. Patton, he's the smartest snake they ever was."

No one disagreed.

Buck slept in the shed, near the cage. Ezry checked on Patton every morning before leaving for the mine, and visited each evening to watch the slow moving rattler.

Berthy did not give in. Annie and Suse were not allowed near the shed, and there was no talk of Patton at the supper table.

"Hit's bad enough," she told her sister, "to be having a rattle-snake right on yer place. But they ain't bringin him, ner no talk of 'im, into my house."

At every opportunity she asked Ezry to get rid of the rattler.

"I'm tellin ye, Ezry," she swore, "someday that things gonna git loose and kill one of the babies. You're gonna be one sorry man, Ezry Hall, that you ever brung that snake to this house."

"Dang it, Berthy," Ezry finally said, "I'm tired o' listenin to you. Jist hush up and let that old snake be. He'll die afore winter, more'n likely, so I don't want to hear nothin else."

†††††

Suse, the baby, four years old, desperately longed to be a part of the excitement.

Ezry was firm. "Yer Mam said no, Suse. You jist keep away from the crib, honey, and keep yer Mam happy."

"But I love Patton," argued Suse. "And you *said* he's a pet. Kin I pet him, Pap?"

"Lord, no," Ezry said wearily. "*Nobody* pets Patton."

"Ovey does," said Suse, "he told me so."

"No he don't," said Ezry. "He's funnin you, Suse. That's all."

The next morning Suse confronted Ovey with Ezry's statement.

"I do so pet Patton!" yelled Ovey. "Jist me! He's my friend. Nobody else gits to pet 'im, neither, not even Pap." He strode away proudly, chest thrust forward, chin jutting.

Jody caught Suse as she followed. "Suse, you ain't sposed to go near the crib. Mam said. She'll whup your bottom iffen she ketches you goin down there. Sides, its jist a old snake. It ain't nothin."

"Ovey gits to pet Patton," whimpered Suse. "I wanta pet

'im too."

Later, carrying her kitten, she slipped away to the shed. She opened the door and slipped inside. Patton's tail buzzed, and Suse stared. The kitten clawed free and ran.

Suse walked closer, her hand out. "Good old Patton," she crooned. "You're a good boy, Patton."

The rattler swayed, tongue flicking. "Nice Patton," she said. "I brung you some grass."

He struck, tangling his fangs in the wire.

Suse smiled.

"Patton likes to play. I'll play with you, Patton."

†††††††

"Where's Suse?" asked Berthy.

"Off somewheres with them cats, I reckon," said Jody.

"Find her," said Berthy. "It's time to eat."

Buck yawned, scratched, and followed Jody to the barnyard.

Near the crib he froze, ears pointed, growled, and charged the door.

"Stop, Buck," wailed Jody. "Don't you hurt Pap's old snake."

He followed, running.

Berthy heard Suse scream, grabbed a hoe and ran, praying.

Jody was standing in the door.

Buck, his teeth firmly clamped on the tail of Suse's short dress, was tugging, growling, pulling her back. The open cage lay on the ground, and Patton's rattles were singing.

Jody shoved Suse out the door. Buck ran back, barking frantically, circling the cage. Patton's head was outside the cage.

Ovey pushed through. "Git, Buck!" he screamed. "Git away from my snake, you durn ol dog."

Jody caught Buck and dragged him outside. "Come outa there, Ovey," he ordered.

"No!" screeched Ovey. "I'm ketchin Patton."

Berthy, assured that Suse was safe, advanced, hoe raised.

"Ovey's in there," said Jody, "and he won't come out."

Berthy stepped cautiously inside.

"Stop, Mam," whispered Ovey. She did.

Ovey squatted three feet from the rattler, talking quietly.

"Lay back down, Patton," he said. "Ain't nobody gonna hurt you none. Git on back in yer cage, Patton."

The buzzing slowed. "Git back, Patton," urged Ovey, "so I kin shut up the door."

Slowly, Patton retreated. Even more slowly, Ovey used a stick to shut the door. Berthy sagged to the ground, her knees trembling. Ovey lifted the cage back to the barrel top.

"We got 'im, Mam," he finally said.

"Praise the Lord," said Berthy.

"I petted Patton, I petted Patton," sang Suse.

Berthy slumped against the wall and cried.

††††††

Ezry came home to a wall of silence.

He washed off the coal dust, changed clothes, and sat at the table, "Alright," he finally asked, "what happened?"

"Yore snake," spat Berthy, "like to killed Suse."

"He didn't neither," wailed Ovey. "She was botherin 'im."

"I petted Patton," Suse said proudly.

Ezry's head dropped to his hands. "Son," he said quietly, "the snake's gotta go."

"NO, Pap," screamed Ovey. "He's mine. He's my onliest friend. You can't take 'im, you can't!" He ran, sobbing, out the door.

Ezry walked slowly to the crib, sat on a sack of feed, and watched the slithering movement in the cage.

"Ovey," he said, "if we was to put on a lock, on the door, and you was to promise to watch Suse, maybe . . ."

"Please, Pap?" Ovey was at his feet, begging.

The heavy padlock was hung in half an hour.

Berthy's frown greeted Ezry. "You're lettin 'im keep it, ain't you?"

"I am," said Ezry. "Berthy, hits locked up, now. Ain't nobody but me and Ovey got a key."

"He nigh kilt your baby," Berthy said softly.

"He never," answered Ezry. "And sendin 'im off, that'd about kill Ovey."

✝✝✝✝✝✝

For a month Berthy fretted.

She could not rest easy if Suse was outside, and she worried that Ovey would accidently release the rattler during the hours he spent in the crib. She decided to fight back.

In the barn she found a curling length of slim hose, and carried it with her to the house. She found Jody's marbles, in the Bull Durham sack, and shook them. She smiled, and tied the bag to the hose. She pulled down the quilt, slipped the hose into Ezry's bed, and covered the lump with a sheet. She shook the bed, listened to the clicking marbles, and smiled.

Supper was ready when Ezry came home.

Berthy was quiet and thoughtful during the meal. "What's botherin you?" asked Ezry.

"I been wonderin," said Berthy. "Iffen that snake got loose, he'd come right in the house, I bet, and git in one of the youngens' beds."

Ezry laughed nervously. "He ain't gittin loose, Berthy."

"But what if he did?"

Ezry shook his head and rolled a cigarette.

Suse helped. "Pap," she said, climbing to his knee, "I bet iffen Patton got loose he'd come and sleep with me."

Ezry's laugh was strained.

Before bedtime Ovey checked the cage three times.

"Can snakes climb?" asked Suse.

"Some," said Ezry, "Why?"

"When Patton gits loose he's gonna come and climb right up in my bed," said Suse. "And I'm gonna hug 'im."

"He can't git loose," Ezry swore hoarsly.

After the children were in bed Berthy brought out her quilting and worked quietly.

"I'm goin to bed," announced Ezry.

"You go on," said Berthy. "I'm goin to set here and piece some more."

She smiled. "Ezry, *can* snakes climb?"

"No, dadburn it, snakes can't climb!"

"Good." Berthy sniffed, and went back to her quilting. Ezry closed the door, and the lights went out.

A frantic bellow rocked the cabin.

Berthy ran to the bedroom door.

Ezry was fighting the sheets, yelling and ripping, and the marbles clicked wildly. He hit the floor, grabbed sheet and quilt and slung them through the closed window. Glass shattered, Buck came roaring, and Ezry grabbed the shotgun.

"Wait, Ezry," yelled Berthy.

She was too late. He fired, leaning out the window, and the smoke filled the room.

"What's happenin?" screamed Jody.

"It's that snake," wailed Ezry.

"Don't you hurt Patton!" screeched Ovey. He grabbed a lantern and ran to the crib.

Jody wrestled Buck to the floor.

"I declare," said Berthy, "all this commotion over a little snake." She returned to the quilt.

Half an hour later Ezry kicked at the clump and jumped back.

"Git me a stick," he yelled. "I found 'im."

He probed cautiously, then walked to the light.

"That ain't no snake, Pap," said Annie. "You done kilt your old hose."

"Patton ain't hurt," yelled Ovey. "He's here in the cage."

Ezry shook his head, sat on the edge of the porch, and stared glumly into the darkness.

†††††††

For two weeks Ezry could not talk to Berthy. He ate in silence, packed his own lunches, and even snapped at Suse, who ran crying. He kicked Buck, and did not go near the crib.

Late Tuesday of the third week Ezry had to brake hard to miss Ovey, who came running from the bushes, blocking the road.

"Gosh durn," grumbled Ezry. "I about kilt you, Ovey. What in tarnation are you doin?"

Ovey's face was pale. "It's Patton. He's loose."

"Lord," said Ezry. "When did he git out?"   ·

"He was gone this mornin," said Ovey. "I been huntin all day."

Ovey trembled. "Maybe he went home, Pap."

"Maybe he never," said Ezry. "Git in, Ovey. We got us some huntin to do."

At the cabin he was brief. "Berthy, git Annie and Suse in the house. Keep 'em there." He frowned. "Hit's that snake," he admitted. "He's loose somewheres." He loaded the shotgun. "Jody, git Buck, and the axe."

"I'm comin too, Pap," said Ovey. "When we find Patton I'll ketch 'im."

"Ovey," said Ezry. "When I find that rattler I'm killin him. That's that. You wait here."

They searched the barn, crib, henhouse, and the surrounding brush. "I reckon he's left," said Ezry, "or Buck woulda found 'im."

†††††††

Suse woke up screaming in the night, bringing Ezry up the ladder with the shotgun. Outside, Buck barked fiercely.

"Jist a dream, honey," said Ezry. He leaned out the window. "Shut up, Buck, you sorry hound. If you was any account youda done found that rattlesnake."

Buck, cowering, *had* found Patton.

He whimpered, dug at the rocks around the cabin, and finally sat guard and waited for morning.

††††††

The fat rattler, sluggish and content, lay curled in the warm dust under the cabin.

During the previous night a rat, feeding in the crib, strayed close to the cage. Patton struck, shook the door open, and attacked. He swallowed the rat whole, and found a warm, dry place to digest his fresh supper.

††††††

Throughout the next day Buck sat, mournfully guarding over the stone foundation. He refused to run with Jody or visit with Suse in her playhouse, and he did not eat. He sat, patient, waiting.

Ezry was home at four. "Pap," asked Jody, "is Buck sick? He won't do nothin but set. Jist looks under the house and whines some. You reckon he's et somethin rotten?"

"I dunno," said Ezry. "He's a actin awful funny."

"Buck misses Patton," chirped Suse. "Buck's lonesome, and he wants Patton to come and play."

"Lord!" shouted Ezry. "That's it! Buck's found 'im. Where's yer Mam?"

"Down in the garden," said Annie.

"Go tell her," said Ezry, "that we found the snake." He ran for the shotgun. "Git away from the house, all of ye."

Buck licked his ear as Jody leaned to peer under the house.

"Stop it, Buck," he complained. "Git away."

The dog pulled at Jody's pants leg, growling.

Ovey, wailing, dug at the rocks. "You ain't gonna shoot my Patton," he sobbed. "I'm gittin 'im out."

Ezry caught the boy, held him aloft, and handed him to Berthy, who arrived out of breath, still carrying her hoe. "Hold 'im," said Ezry.

Under the cabin Patton squirmed to life. He buzzed briefly, then searched for an escape route. He found a hole, poked his head through, and crawled outside.

Buck met him.

Patton coiled, swaying to strike, and Buck feinted. Ovey broke away and was the first to arrive.

"Git, Buck," he yelled. "Leave my snake alone."

Jody shoved Ovey across the yard, and waited for Buck to jump clear. The hound darted, drew the strike, spun away, and yelped in angry surprise as Jody grabbed his tail and threw him tumbling after Ovey. Ezry grabbed Buck and held him back.

"Got 'im!" yelled Ezry. "Come and hold 'im, Jody."

Patton's tail blurred as Ezry leveled the shotgun.

"No, Pap, please." Ovey tugged at the barrels. "Please don't shoot Patton, Pap."

Ezry hesitated, then lowered the gun slightly. "If he leaves," he said, "I won't shoot. He starts back under the house I'll kill 'im."

Patton was battle ready, coiled, swaying, buzzing.

After a minute he slithered away, past the rosebush and across the dusty yard.

"He's goin, Pap. He's leavin." Ovey jumped with joy.

Patton slid slowly across the yard, moving toward the brush. He followed the footpath, passing the chickens, nearing the outhouse, fat body tracking in the dust.

The steel flashed.

From behind the outhouse Berthy attacked, hoe whipping,

apron billowing.

Ovey screamed and ran to her. Patton twitched in the loose dirt.

Berthy shouldered the hoe, turned, and marched to the cabin without speaking.

Suse followed. "Mam," she asked, "ain't you gonna warsh off the hoe?"

†††††

The grave was long and narrow, and Ovey solemnly conducted the services.

Suse and Annie sang "Rock Of Ages," and Buck whimpered appropriately. Ezry's bayonet was the marker; Jody fired two shots from the 12 gauge.

Patton was laid to rest with full military honors.

†††††

"Ovey," said Ezry, "I'll git you another pet."

"Don't want none," sniffed Ovey. "Sides, Mam'd kill it too."

"Yer Mam, she was skeered Patton'd bite one of the little uns. She was right too. He'd a kilt anything come close enough."

Ovey grinned evilly. "He woulda, wouldn't he?" He wiggled his toes in the dust. " 'Cept fer Mam."

Ezry chuckled. "She's sumpin else, yer Mam is. She's a lot like old Patton was. She ain't skeered o' nothin, Ovey."

"She ain't, is she? Jist like Patton." He giggled. "Mam, and Patton. Both meaner'n the Devil." He leaped to his feet, still grinning. "Jist like Patton," he repeated. "Both of em is mighty fierce, Pap."

"They shore are, Ovey."

"I reckon they had to fight someday."

"Reckon so."

"Well." Ovey was silent. "I guess the bestun won."

When school started Ovey carried his newspaper clippings, boasting of his pet rattler, telling fearsome tales of deadly fangs and lightning speed.

"But I'll tell ye," he whispered to the group of awed boys, "Mam, she wasn't skeered, none at all. He got loose, Patton did, and almost kilt Jody and Pap. Mam, she snuck up and took the hoe to 'im, kilt him right there. Chopped him." He snapped his fingers. "Jist like that. She's some fierce, my Mam is." His chest swelled. "My Mam ain't afraid o' nothing."

††††††

Berthy looked up from the chopping block.

"Ovey, what's all them boys doin here gawkin at me?"

She flipped the axe, burying it to the shaft, and turned. The boys scattered, fearful, stopping to stare with admiring eyes.

Ovey strutted slowly after them.

††††††

"Ezry," she said, "that Ovey, he's got to actin plum funny. Sneakin and grinnin at me, and today he brung a bunch of boys home from school. Why, they acted downright skeered o' me. Whatsa matter, you reckon?"

"Berthy June," grinned Ezry, "That boy's found 'im somethin else to be proud of. Jist like Patton, to his way o' lookin at things." He chuckled as he rolled the cigarette. "Yessir, jist like Patton."

"Law, Ezry Hall, sometimes you do act plum crazy."

"Ain't that the truth," chuckled Ezry. He hugged Berthy and she blushed. "That shore is the gospel truth."

THE BURYING OF WEBSTER MacFARLAND

Webster Daniel MacFarland, a prolific moonshiner for most of his eighty-four years, died peacefully, asleep in the attic bedroom of his weathered cabin near the headwaters of Upper Toenail Creek near Brown Mountain. It was two days before Jimmy MacFarland, a grandson, found the body and galloped back down the steps to summon his father, Luster, from the muddy pickup truck parked in the yard.

"Come a runnin," he gasped. "Grandpap, I reckon he's done kicked the bucket." He hung his head mournfully. "He don't say nothin, and he's mighty swole up."

"Dagnabit," swore Luster. He spat angrily into the wind which whipped across the ridge. "I was needin to git some shine and borry me some cash money from 'im." He sighed wearily. "I guess you're wantin me to go look at him?"

Luster casually inspected Webster. "Yep. Deader'n Hell." He bent to search the old man's pockets. "Well, git busy, dammit, and see if ye can find any money here." Luster and Jimmy methodically searched the cluttered cabin, jerking drawers open and throwing papers and clothing across the floors. They found no cash, no negotiable papers, and no records of where Webster had stashed his latest drippings. Luster swore, gave up, and drove down off the ridge to inform the coroner and the rest of the MacFarland family.

The direct descendants of Webster MacFarland were scattered and plentiful. An energetic and astoundingly fertile breeder, Webster had outlasted three exhausted wives in fathering 21 offspring, a melange of full and half siblings who populated most of Brown Mountain and had made a healthy start at taking over the Ohio mill town where a group of sons had migrated after the war. The most recent tally, done by a grandaughter as a classroom project, reflected 214 grandchildren, almost 300 great-grandchildren, and a smattering of expectant mothers, wed and unwed, ready to pad the totals at any moment.

The eldest sister from the original wife was Mary Magdalene Rose, and to her fell the burden of dispersing the news to the rest of the scattered MacFarlands. She consulted her list, and started calling in chronological order. For seven hours she dialed the collect calls, a grim bearer of ill tidings, a shrill death messenger who gloried in her role as matriarch of the bereaved clan.

Mary Magdalene issued orders with a voice of undisputed authority. The nine original offspring would gather at her house. The second group, seven in number, were to congregate at Willie's place just over the mountain. The final five were directed to gather at Roseanna's. Then, as a group, they would merge at the homeplace cabin.

The local MacFarlands began digging out their extra blankets and pillows, carrying in canned goods and cured hams from the smokehouses, baking pies and cakes and loaves of bread, and a whole side of beef was buried in a charcoal pit. They aired out the funeral outfits of black musty wool and polished the Sunday shoes and boots. A holiday mood swept Brown Mountain; there was a noisy rushing and chattering as the MacFarlands readied themselves for Webster's burying.

At Watson's Funeral Home the body was duly washed, embalmed, combed and powdered, and laid out formally in an ill-fitted, cheap black suit. For the first time in twenty years Webster's white beard was clean and untangled, free from its streaks of dried tobacco juice. The mortician was able to fashion a morbid smile, and told his assistant that Webster'd be happy to know that his veins were now filled with pure alcohol, more potent even than the 180 proof corn he'd distilled and sold for most of his life.

The coffin was of ornate brass and rosewood, befitting the fallen leader of a clan rooted in Scottish mysticism and the bloody memories of the Brown Mountain War between the MacFarlands and the Coxes.

At rest, ready for display, Webster Daniel MacFarland was an imposing, waxy figure, a heroic mountain warrior prepared to receive his final tribute.

†††††

Luster returned to the cabin and resumed his search. The barn, the haystacks, the root cellar, the chickenhouse, the hogpens, the crib, and the woodpile were sterile grounds. There was no money, no moonshine, nothing to satisfy Luster's impatient thirst.

"The old son of a gun," he grumbled. "He hid it all sommers, and I aim to find it afore them others gits here. Damnit, Jimmy, where'd Pap put stuff?"

"I dunno," said Jimmy. "We done looked everwhere I know of. He musta found him a new hidin place."

Luster found his flask and took a long, gargling pull, gasped, and wiped his lips. "It'd be jist like him," he grumbled. "Probly knowed he was dyin and went out and hid everthing sommers where I ain't never gonna find it."

Jimmy poked gingerly at a pile of shavings, anxiously watching for copperheads. "Let's go on home, Pap," he said. "Fergit about it."

"I can't fergit," said Luster. "I need the money."

†††††

By noon the crowds were gathering.

Dusty cars with Ohio licenses and loaded seats rolled noisily into the county, each tracking off to the proper meeting house, each representing one of the branches of Webster's family. The lines were clearly drawn. Three sets of children decided Webster would be buried beside *their* mother; three graves were ordered dug and readied.

The first family meeting was set for four o'clock at the homeplace, and each branch would arrive determined to win.

Nineteen year old Elroy, the baby of Jimmy's seven offspring, was a redfaced and curly haired youngster with a gangly body and a ready grin, and had been the favorite of Webster MacFarland. Of all the family, Elroy was the most grieved, the most anxious to see that his great-grandfather's memory was properly honored. Elroy, even as a small child, had spent days with the old man, keeping him company in the dusky cabin, helping with the chores, walking with him on the mountain, hoeing the garden, helping pour off the clear liquid from the MacFarland still near the creek. Elroy loved Webster with a fierce and protective passion, and he angrily stomped away from his aunts and uncles and cousins who were so openly enjoying the unexpected reunion.

Elroy drove his old red pickup to the homeplace, and sat mournfully, slumped on the worn porch, wallowing in his sorrow.

Janis found him there, and joined him. She too was troubled by the family's reaction, and had slipped quietly away to mourn Webster's death. Twenty-two and single, Janis was Elroy's co-worker at the shoe factory and his closest friend. She wore cutoff jeans and a faded T shirt, and her presence lifted Elroy's weary spirits. Janis joined him on the porch, sat down, and scooted across the smooth boards to perch beside him. Her hands were wrapped around her ankles, her head on her knees, and finally she spoke.

"Hi, Elroy." The voice was husky and subdued.

"Howdy, Janis." Elroy was still unsure of his new deep basso and spoke carefully to avoid the embarrassing squeaks and rumbles. "My family still argyin over who's gonna git what?"

"Yeah." She sighed. "And eatin. Lord, Elroy, I ain't never seen so much food. Don't any of 'em seem to care about Webster bein dead."

"I do." Tears clouded Elroy's sad eyes.

"I know it, Elroy." Janis leaned closer and quickly kissed him, on the ear. Elroy jerked away, blushing. He sweated profusely and tried to not stare.

Janis giggled. "You're cute, Elroy." Her hand carressed his neck. "Do I make you nervous?"

'N-no," he stammered. "It's jist the weather."

She moved closer. Elroy felt her breath and squirmed. "I jus feel so awful," sighed Janis. "Elroy, do you know how you could make me feel better?"

"H-how?" He twisted to face her.

Janis smiled. She stood, bent to help Elroy to his feet, and led him to the door. His hoarse wheezing filled the little room, familiar with its strong smells of tobacco and lard, and Elroy stumbled as Janis came to him in a rush, whimpering as she pressed close. Elroy growled, lifted her off the floor, and squeezed. She squealed.

"Lordy, Elroy, don't kill me!"

Chastened, he dropped her and backed away.

Janis smiled and slid back into his arms, then screeched and tore herself away as a musical car horn blared "Dixie" from the front yard. "Oh, damn," she spat, "It's your uncle." She ran, shorts tangled over her hips, wiggling as she fled, and ducked into the attic.

Buck MacFarland found Elroy, red and sweaty, flopped on Webster's worn sofa with his legs crossed.

"Howdy, Uncle Buck," whispered Elroy.

Janis, from the top of the stairs, smiled.

"Is it already time for your meeting?"

††††††

It was time.

A dozen vehicles arrived and parked in the barren yard of Webster's cabin; twenty of his twenty-one progeny were present.

"Where's Luster?" asked Mary Magdalene.

"Out in his truck," grunted Buck. "Probably passed out drunk."

"Go git him," she ordered. "Willie, you and Roseanna, you come over here and set with me." She tucked her skirts primly and folded her fat arms under massive breasts.

Luster, mumbling darkly, poked his head through the door. He nodded, to acknowledge the presence of his brothers and sisters, then glowered at Mary Magdalene. "What in tarnation do ye want now?" he growled. "I got stuff I need to be doin."

She sniffed. "Don't ye think, Luster, that ye could stop huntin fer pap's whiskey long enough to help us figger out the buryin?"

"God Damn," said Luster. "Is that what ye drug me in her fer? Hell, dig a hole and lay him in it. He wouldn't give one damn what ye do."

"Well, I never!" Roseanna snapped to her feet, huffing and swelling. "Luster MacFarland, you ain't got no respect."

Luster blinked and stared. "How come you actin like a old settin hen? You never done nothin fer him whilst he was alive, and he never liked you none noway."

"You-You-." Redfaced, sputtering and swinging, Roseanna attacked.

Luster firmly caught both flailing fists, guided her to a chair, sat her down hard and turned to face the crowd. "I'll be goin," he said. "I got better to do than set here squabblin over a dead man's dead wives." He left, swaggering and swaying.

"Old sot," sniffed Roseanna, wiping at her swollen eyes. "And, *he* was Pap's favorite, too."

"Let's git on with it," said Mary Magdalene. She cleared her throat violently and sat erect in her chair. Her voice was that of unquestionable authority. "The buryin is day after tomorrow. Tonight we'll all set with him. After the service we'll come on out here fer the buryin up on the mountain, beside mamma."

"J-jist a m-minute," protested Willie. Frail and arthritic, he was slow to his feet. "W-we're gonna bury Pap n-next to *our* mother." His six siblings nodded vigorous agreement.

Roseanna squalled. "You ain't neither. He was married with *our* mamma last." She jumped up, angry and excited, bumped into Willie and sent him toppling into Mary Magdalene's ample lap. He bounced, gasped, and staggered backwards. Buck sighed, reached out a strong arm, caught Willie and guided him firmly back to the sofa.

"We done got a grave bein dug," said Roseanna. "He'll be laid next to our mother."

"We're diggin one too," snapped Mary Magdalene.

"U-us too," stammered Willie, struggling to rise again.

Buck held him down. Roseanna screeched angrily, slapped Buck, and for her efforts was repaid with a quick left to the nose. Mary Magdalene shoved Ellie into Willard, who fell and kicked over Jack's rickety chair and dumped him, sound asleep, into the floor. Margie promptly slapped Allan, who whacked her back across the room and into Willie's lap. Mary Magdalene bit her while she sat, and the battle was joined in earnest.

A shrill bloodletting rocked the fieldstone foundations of Webster's cabin, flushed a flock of birds into screeching flight, and sent Webster's old hound, tail tucked, running desperately for shelter. A sleeping fox, startled awake, ran crookedly across the porch, heard the wails, barked, laid his ears back and ran for the safety of the deepest forest.

†††††††

Janis slipped her arm through Elroy's and led him away.

"Fools!" he growled angrily. "Goddamned old fools!"

His long strides dragged Janis to the old jeep truck.

"I know what Grandpappy wanted," he sobbed. "I'll fix them, by God. I will, Janis. You jist watch."

"Elroy, what in the world are you gonna do?"

Tears streamed down his red cheeks. "You'll see."

"Elroy. I . . I'll help you."

He peered at her. "You sure?"

"Yes."

"It ain't gonna be . . . they ain't gonna like it, what I'm gonna do."

"It don't matter, Elroy." Janis smiled. "I said I'd help you."

"You be ready, then. About ten tonight?"

"Ready for what, Elroy?"

"I'll tell ye then. I got to do some work."

"OK." She smiled tenderly. "Elroy, don't you go and git in no trouble. I . . . I like you a lot, Elroy."

"I'll git you at ten," he snapped.

†††††††

The Watson Brothers Funeral Home, a staid three story former residence with white paint and neat green trim, was silent. Webster MacFarland's ornate casket lay in state, banked by a profusion of floral arrangements, massive in the dim parlor.

Harold Watson fretted, twisting his limp wrists, mentally rechecking his preparations for the MacFarland onslaught, and the persistent hammering at the door jarred him back to reality. He quickly flicked on the tape recorder, and muted organ music filled the room. He straightened his tie, and walked somberly to unlock the front door. Luster MacFarland, grinning happily, stumbled across the doorjamb.

"Howdy, Harold," he croaked. "Am I the onliest one here?"

"You are the first of many," intoned Harold. His voice was properly pastoral.

"We better git us a crosscut saw afore them others gits here," drawled Luster. "You and me'll cut Pap into three pieces."

"What?" Harold was discreetly shocked.

"Damndest fight I ever seen," chuckled Luster. "Men a hittin wimmen, clothes a gittin tore off, screamin and kickin and bitin and clawin—."

"What *are* you talking about, Luster?"

"You ain't heerd? Hell, the MacFarlands is fightin over who gits the body. 'Pears to me they all got whupped, and they are a sorry lookin bunch right now. They done went and dug three graves, and when I left they was lookin to need several more."

Harold coughed politely, chewing his lower lip, covering his mouth with a scented handkerchief. "I'm sure they've settled their differences by now," he said.

"I ain't so damn sure," laughed Luster. "They was some powerful hollerin and cussin goin on. We orta saw Pap in two, Harold." He chuckled softly, then brushed past Watson and walked to the coffin to stand in reverent silence. His shoulders were slumped, his head bowed. Harold joined him.

"He was a *good* man," he said.

"Best God Damn moonshiner in ten counties," sobbed Luster. "His stuff, hit was always clean and at least a hunnert and eighty proof. He never used no lye, and he never cut it more'n twice."

"He was . . . I'm sure . ." Watson fumbled. "I'm sure he was very good at . . . at what he did, Luster."

"Good?" Luster's voice climbed. "Hell, he was the best! Lotsa folks gonna miss 'im, come drinkin time." He dried his eyes and blew his nose loudly. "I jist wisht to hell he'd a told me where he hid everthing afore he died."

He cut a chew and held it, thoughtful. "By God," he exclaimed. "They's one place I ain't looked yit!"

He ran to the door. "Hey, Harold," he yelled, "tell them damn brothers and sisters o' mine I been here and left." He was outside, in his truck and rolling, when Mary Magdalene's big Pontiac made the turn into the lot and lurched as she stabbed the brake. Luster swerved, swore, shook his fist at her and roared past.

She parked, got out, and stared after the rattling, smoking pickup, then went inside. "Was that Luster that jist left?" she asked.

"Yes'm, Miz Rose," said Watson. "It shore was."

"Was he drunk?"

"No, ma'am," said Harold. "Not so's you'd notice."

Mary Magdalene drew her shoulders erect. "What are you gawkin at, Harold?" she asked.

He blushed. "Nothin, Miz Rose. Nothin at all." Her left eye was swollen shut, purple and puffy. She walked with a slight limp, favoring the left hip. "I fell down," she snapped. "Are you done lookin?"

"Yes, Miz Rose. I mean I . . . come on in and set down. Let me git you some fresh coffee."

The other MacFarlands arrived in maternal clusters, sulky and tightlipped, some walking stiffly from concealed bruises and two in slings, Willie with a neat bandage around his head and Buck rubbing sore knuckles. The three sets of Webster's offspring established separate calling areas, refused to speak to each other, and friends of the family noted a slight air of hostility in the musty parlor.

††††††

Elroy finished loading the jeep, drove to Janis' house at nine-thirty, and parked at the door. He knocked and Janis, dripping around the bulky towel, answered.

"Oh, it's you." She smiled. "I just got out of the shower. Come on in, Elroy."

"You . . . " He gulped. "You ain't go no clothes on, Janis."

She smiled again. "I wondered if you'd ever notice, Elroy. Come a little closer."

He edged over. The towel fluttered, and Elroy's breath was sucked away. He watched the terrycloth down to the floor, then slowly, slowly raised his eyes.

†††††

Luster was driving frantically, swerving to miss the traffic and keep the truck on the rutted roadway, and he jerked the wheel hard when he found the little lane that led to the MacFarland homeplace. He slid the truck to a shuddering stop, slammed the door and ran, plowing up through the thick underbrush of Brown Mountain.

†††††

Elroy swallowed, and tried to pull his thick tongue back in place. "I . . . Janis, I . . ."

She stood, hands on her hips, eyes shining, smiling.

"Elroy? Are you OK?"

"Yep." His voice cracked and squeaked.

"Do you like the way I look?"

"L-Lord, yes, Janis." His face burned, and his big hands threatened to rip out his pockets. "But, I . . We . . . damnit, Janis, they ain't time."

"No time? Elroy, are you crazy?"

"No, ma'am, I ain't." His dry mouth slowed his tongue. "But, we got to—to do stuff."

She stared. "OK," she finally muttered. "OK, Elroy, what is it?" She bent to retrieve the towel.

"Git some work clothes on," said Elroy. "We'll be liftin."

"Just what are we gonna do?"

"I'll show you," said Elroy. "Hurry up now."

Janis slung the towel over her shoulder and looked back over her shoulder. "You sure you wouldn't rather stay here a while?"

"H-hurry," grunted Elroy. He jammed his hands deeper and walked stiffly away. Janis giggled and went for clothes.

She combed her hair as he drove, too fast, the old jeep groaning its protest, to the hill overlooking the Watson Brothers Funeral Home. He parked, and let the boiling engine cool, waiting in the shadows for the last of the visitors to leave.

"You sure you want to do this, Elroy?" asked Janis. "It's awful—dangerous, and—." She shivered—"gruesome."

"Hit's fer Grandpappy," Elroy said solemnly.

✝✝✝✝✝✝

From halfway up the steep slope of Brown Mountain the happy and well oiled voice of Luster MacFarland crackled as he sang his nasal monotone. He was stretched flat across a protruding ledge, an empty quart jar beside him, a roll of bills scattered around. He had found his treasure.

Webster MacFarland's cache of aging moonshine, his tin strongbox of working capital, his recipe, and his list of prime customers were now Luster's. Hidden under the overhanging rock, concealed by thick brush, the little cave had been Webster's office. Once a playground for the children, the cave had been forgotten for decades, except by the old man who coveted its privacy. For three decades the cave had been Webster's sanctuary, his refuge from his everpresent and unpleasant family, his office and counting room, his warehouse, and often his bedroom. The cave was safe, a secure storage shed for the moonshine, free from the probing law officers and Luster's thirst.

Elroy had shared the secret of the cave with Webster; he alone was aware of the old man's hillside executive suite and warehouse.

Luster's memory had been jogged by the fight. Always, when

he tired of the bickering and whining, Webster had retreated up the mountain. Luster had finally made the connection, and the cave was providing a rich reward.

Now, a new quart open and the cash littered around him, Luster celebrated and mourned, alone on the dark mountain.

††††††

The last light was turned off and Harold Watson carefully bolted the big double door. He stopped, fifty feet away, for a proud look back at his prize possession, then whistled as he walked homeward.

Elroy started the jeep and drove cautiously to the rear entrance. He backed the jeep close to the loading dock, and used heavy oak boards to build a ramp.

"Lord, Elroy," whispered Janis, "don't do it. They'll hang you for stealin a corpse."

Elroy just grinned. The window slipped open easily, and he wriggled inside to open the door. He led Janis down a dark corridor to the parlor, where Webster lay in proud silence. The coffin lid was closed.

"This here thing's got wheels," said Elroy. "Help me push."

Puffing, cursing softly, nervous, they rolled the coffin to the dock and slid it onto the truck. Elroy draped a tarp over the bulk.

"We got him," said Janis. "Let's git out of here."

"Not jist yit," whispered Elroy. He found another bronzed coffin, empty, loaded it on the cart, and wheeled it to the parlor. "Git them flowers back like they was," he ordered. They rearranged the stately display and slipped quietly out the back, locking the door as they went.

After a half mile Janis sighed with relief. "It's done," she said. "Fer better or worse."

"Hell," said Elroy. "We ain't done. That was the easy part."

He drove to the homeplace cabin, passed it, and found the

overgrown logging road. He put the jeep in four wheel drive, and the grinding gears and laboring engine shattered the night silence.

"Where *are* we goin?" asked Janis, clinging to the bouncing dashboard.

"Bout another half of a mile," grunted Elroy. "I'm a takin Grandpap to his favorite place."

The staggering headlights and struggling engine caught Luster's attention. He crawled to his feet, ran inside the cave, and came back levering a cartridge into the firing chamber of Webster's old .30-.30 carbine. "God Damn revenooers," he muttered. He flopped to his stomach, flat against the ledge, and waited.

The lights were within a hundred yards. Luster frowned, sighted carefully, and squeezed the trigger.

A headlight exploded. The copper clad slug slammed through the rusted metal and into a slick tire, caromed away with a buzz and the hiss of leaking air. Janis wailed. Elroy shut off the engine and dragged her out the door, tumbling hard in the sticky brambles. He covered her with his body and pressed flat.

"Somebody shot at us," moaned Janis. "I told you we shouldn't a done this."

Elroy was gulping for air, and thinking. "It's Luster. It's gotta be Uncle Luster, drunker'n hell."

"Find out, damnit, before he kills us both," squalled Janis.

Elroy inched forward and cupped his hands. "Luster? Uncle Luster? Are you up there?"

There was silence.

"Uncle Luster?"

"That you, Elroy?"

"Hit's me. Can we come up?"

"We? Who in hell's with you?"

"Janis."

"Oh." The pause was a half minute long. "OK. I thought

ye was the law."

Elroy and Janis climbed slowly, cautiously, until they saw Luster in the darkness.

"What in the hell are you a doin here?" asked Luster.

Elroy squatted beside his uncle and sipped from the open jar. He smacked his lips, and grinned. "I brung Grandpappy."

Luster stared. He turned to Janis. "Is Elroy bad drunk?"

"I'm afraid not," she said. "Webster's in the jeep."

"Lord have mercy! Did ye steal him?"

"Wasn't stealin, exactly," said Elroy. "They was all a fightin over where to put 'im, and I knowed where he wanted to be."

"I'll be damned." Luster drank deeply, and blinked. "So ye jist stoled him."

"I reckon so," Elroy said glumly. "Are you gonna tell?"

"Nope." Luster sat solidly, and sipped again. "Hell, it makes good sense to me. I reckon you'll be needin some help, though."

Elroy eased the limping jeep closer to the cave. Two hours later the exhausted trio slid the massive coffin into the cave and rested.

"Son of a bitch," groaned Luster. "Couldn't ye a laid 'im down the mountain a ways?"

"Nope. This here was his place."

"How are ye gonna dig a grave?"

"I ain't." Elroy pointed. "I'm gonna slide them rocks up there right down over the cave."

"Seal it off?"

"Yep."

"But—what about the stuff? They must be forty gallon layin in there."

Elroy grinned. "Grandpap'll be needin it. They say hit's mighty hot and dry where he's at."

††††††

Harold Watson opened the big front doors at 9:30 AM, smiling contentedly as he mentally computed the profits from the burying of Webster MacFarland. Humming, singing happy snatches of hymnal music, he straightened the chairs and emptied the ashtrays, readying the parlor for a full day of busy visitation. He paused to peer curiously at the coffin and the flowers.

"Don't seem hardly the same," he muttered. He shrugged, and returned to his cleaning.

The first family members arrived twenty minutes later. Mary Magdalene led the way, her eye even more discolored. Harold timidly blocked her way.

"Miz Rose," he said meekly, "we need to know somethin. Have youens decided?" He coughed into the back of his hand. "About the grave, I mean. Where it's gonna be?"

"Of course we have," she snapped. "He'll be buried where he belongs, right beside my mother."

"Oh, no, he won't," countered Roseanna. She squared her broad shoulders and readied her big purse for swinging.

"W-what's this?" Willie hobbled closer. "You ain't a b-buryin him nowheres I ain't agreed about."

The MacFarlands gathered in a buzzing circle, and the rising crackle of angry voices almost drowned out Harold's faint cry of dismay.

Buck raised his hand for silence. "What in hell did you say, Harold?"

Harold stumbled away, palefaced and trembling.

"It's Mr. MacFarland," he gasped. "He—he's g-gone."

He fainted, and slowly slid down to rest in the bank of flowers.

††††††

The sun woke Elroy, and he bolted upright.

Then he remembered where he was, and grinned.

Janis stirred under the blanket, uncovering touseled hair and a sleepy face and bare, slender shoulders. "Elroy?" Her voice was a throaty, sleepy purr. "You come back here."

He sat back down, rubbing his sore shoulders, inspecting torn hands. He smiled. "We done it, Janis."

"We sure did." Her smile was lazy, content, and she opened her arms. "Now come back here."

She was nibbling at his chest and neck, still warm and soft from sleeping, melting to him as the birds chattered and the morning sun dried the dew off Brown Mountain.

A hundred yards uphill, Luster clung to a fat oak tree and happily surveyed their night's work. The cave was sealed by a huge boulder. The jeep, sagging to the front, sat close by, tools cast randomly back inside the bed. Webster's rifle was leaned against a rock, near the strongbox, and three dozen full quart bottles were nestled in the deep grass. Four empties snuggled close to Luster. He cuddled a fifth, half empty, close to his body as he rested, swaying gently and singing softly.

††††††

Harold was revived with the help of a gallon of sloshing ice water.

He jerked, sputtered, and stared in terror at the glowering faces above and around him. He tried to rise, worked his lips in an effort to speak, then wilted again.

Buck prodded the limp body with the toe of a heavy boot, and chuckled. "Listen here," he said to the crowd, "he ain't got no corpse, so we don't gotta pay fer no buryin."

"What about pappy?" gasped Roseanna.

"Hell, he was dead anyhow, wasn't he?" Buck grinned and ambled slowly toward the door. The others hesitated, looking at each other, then followed in a mad rush. From the parking lot there came a slamming of doors and roaring of engines as the MacFarlands scattered to rejoin their reunion.

THE PROMISED LAND

The ancient black Ford squatted on rusted springs, badly overloaded, as Luther Cox tightened the frayed rope which held the box springs in place on the roof. He snugged the knot, backed away to rub his hands, and critically studied his ragged handiwork.

"Did you leave a place for Jimmy?" Pale, pregnant Gracie Cox peered intently into the musty interior. "Where's he gonna set, Luther?"

"Gonna be a mite crowded," conceded Luther. "But it ain't for long. Couple of hours, maybe three, we'll be in Cincinnati. Another week or two I'll come back for the rest of our stuff. Soon as we git our own place." He kicked lamely at a bald tire, and scowled. "Better git the pump and air this'n up some," he muttered. "Where's that boy?"

"Over by the smokehouse, I reckon," sighed Gracie. "Him and the dog." She started, hesitated, then finally spoke. "Jimmy, he ain't wantin to leave."

"That ain't for him to say," growled Luther. "We done been through all that. We *got* to go, Gracie. They ain't nothin for us, here." He shrugged. "Jeb shut down the sawmill, they ain't no truckin to be had, not even no coal right now." Luther dug deep in his pocket for the Bull Durham, expertly rolled and licked the cigarette, struck a match on his heel and sucked the smoke deep. "Hell, I'd druther to not be goin," he said softly. "I growed up right here—was borned in the old cabin over yonder—and my people has worked this same land for nigh two hunnert year. But, Gracie, a body can't live no more, not with jist a acre of tobacco and a garden." He dropped the butt and ground it with his heel. "Besides," he grinned, "up in Cincinnati you're gonna have runnin water and a bathroom, and a washin machine, and a electric stove. . .Hell fire, Gracie, ain't you plumb tired of livin like some kind o' heathern? Lordy, woman, we're goin to the promised land."

"It ain't so bad here," whispered Gracie. "We always got plenty food, and a place of our own."

"Yeah," laughed Luther. "Fatback and beans, freezin in the winter, never a damn penny for nothin. No decent school. Up there, they got good schools, Gracie. Jimmy, he can graduate high school, maybe, and git decent work, not have to spend his whole damn life grubbin."

"That part, it's good," agreed Gracie. "I want Jimmy to git a good education. But. . .Elmer and Lucy and all them, *they* ain't doin so good up there. Elmer, he's got to drinkin, and the youngens is jist runnin wild. . ." She bowed her head and clasped her hands over her swollen belly. "With the new one comin, and all. . .I'm skeered, Luther."

Luther's rough hand rested awkwardly, gently, on her thin shoulder. "Don't you go worryin," he said softly. "Fer one thing, I ain't no drinkin man. And Jimmy ain't about to go runnin around. Hell, he's jist nine." He chuckled. "He's done gone plumb wild, right here. Him and that old hound traipsin off all over the hollers, swimmin in the river—he musta got a lot of that Irish blood o' yourn."

Gracie blushed. "Jimmy don't want to have to leave old Sam," she said. "Ain't they some way we can take him with us?"

"Damnation, Gracie," snapped Luther. "I done told you—and Elmer told you—they don't allow no hound dogs in a apartment house. When we can git us a place—out a ways—we'll come back and git the dog. Hell, a month or two, at the most, we can git outa town and find us a little farm. I ain't gonna live in town, not after I git work and save us up some cash. Sam ain't gonna go nowheres. He'll stay right here, with Pap, till we come after him."

"I don't know," sighed Gracie. "Jimmy and old Sam has growed up together."

"Damn dog a sleepin in the house," grumbled Luther, "growlin at me if I so much as raise a hand at the boy. *I* ain't gonna miss that durned hound none."

Gracie giggled. "Don't you remember the time Sam run off that feller from the bank?"

"Yep." Luther grinned. "Saved that old boy from gittin a tail full o' buckshot, too." He took a deep breath. "Time's a wastin, Gracie. Git the boy and let's go."

††††††

"No, sir, Sam, I ain't goin." Jimmy buried his face in the loose folds of the big hound's neck. "I ain't never gonna leave you, Sam. Not never."

Sam whimpered softly, nudged his wet nose under the boy's frail arm, and wormed closer. The oversized black and tan hound, big footed and long tongued, pressed tight to Jimmy and offered wordless comfort. Then, his ears perked and he lifted his nose to sniff. Jimmy twisted. "They're comin," he whispered hoarsely. "Let's git, Sam."

He jerked away, crouched low, and ran for the underbrush. "Come on, Sam," he hissed. "Hurry it up!"

††††††

"Jimmy?" Gracie cupped her hands and yelled. "Jimmy Cox! Where are you?"

Luther joined her, suddenly impatient. "Damnit," he bellowed. "Git here, boy! Right now!"

There was no answer, and Luther's voice echoed off an empty mountainside.

"He's run," grunted Luther. "Him and the dog has gone and hid. ." His face darkened. "I'll go git 'em." He swung into a heavy trot, elbows tight, boots thudding against the hard-packed trail.

"Where you goin?" yelled Gracie.

"To where Jimmy'll be," gasped Luther. "Up in the old rock house."

††††††

Boy and dog broke suddenly through the dense underbrush, splashed across the shallow creek, and sprawled into the mossy darkness of the cavern. Jimmy, gasping, dropped against the wall and hugged the panting hound. "I told you I wasn't goin," he whispered. "They can't make me go, Sam."

Sam thumped happily, licked his master's sweaty face, and curled content against Jimmy's trembling knees.

"I won't leave you, Sam," sobbed Jimmy. "I promise."

Luther Cox approached the rock house slowly, weary now, and stopped short when the low growl rumbled out from the darkness. "It's okay, Sam," he said calmly. "I ain't gonna hurt him none." He waited. "I'm comin in, Jimmy. Call off your dog."

He ducked under the overhang, stood quietly to roll and light a cigarette, then squatted beside the solemn youngster. "I knowed where you'd be," said Luther. "This is where I used to come, when me and Grandpap was fightin."

"Grandpap, he never drug you off to no town," protested Jimmy. "And he never tooken your dog away, neither."

"I'm not takin Sam away, son," said Luther. "He'll be better off here, and pretty soon we'll come and git him. Sam, he wouldn't like livin in Cincinnati."

"Me neither," sobbed Jimmy. "Youens just go on and leave me here. Me and Sam."

"Nope," Luther said softly. "We're all goin, son. You, me,

and your mommy. I take care of my own."

"I don't want to move," said Jimmy.

Luther stiffened. "I damn well don't want to neither, boy. They's lots of things I don't want to do. But, by damn, I do what has to be done, and so will you. You're a Cox. Don't forgit that, Jimmy."

He sucked the last of the cigarette, and stood. "Now, stop the snivelin and come on. Don't let your granddaddy see you actin like a girl."

Sam growled when Luther's hand touched Jimmy, then he tucked his tail and left quickly when he met the cold blue eyes.

They were back at the homeplace in fifteen minutes, Jimmy's face streaked with tears, Luther's leathery features set in a hard scowl. Gracie—and the grandparents—were waiting at the car.

The goodbyes were quaintly formal, physically distant, and oddly strained. The old couple, more stooped, now, quietly watched their youngest son stride quickly to the car and swing open the creaky door. "Load 'em up, son," he yelled to Jimmy. "We got to head north. Let's git, boy. It's gonna be dark by the time we git there."

Jimmy gently rubbed Sam's floppy ears, ran his hands over the worn rope which held the hound close to the gate post, and wiped hot tears. "Goodbye, old Sam," he whispered. "I'll be back to git you." He ran, stumbling, and did not look back.

Luther pushed the starter and the old Ford kicked to life, sputtering and blowing oily smoke, lurching as the gears engaged and the tired engine howled. Down the rutted trail, across the creek at the slick rock, and up the ridge, Luther's moaning sedan kicked up swirling dust clouds and swayed under the heavy load. He stopped at the gravel county road, turned left, worked up through the gears and forced a smile. "We're heaven bound," he said heartily. "Goin to a better life, boy. Come Monday mornin you'll be settin in that brick schoolhouse with all them fancy talkin youngens, and your mommy'll be livin the life of luxury."

Jimmy buried his face in the folds of an old quilt, and Gracie grasped her belly and stared off at the mountaintops. Luther waited for a response.

"Hell fire," he growled. "You two actin like we're goin to a damn funeral."

Neither answered. Luther's fists tightened on the shiny steering wheel, and he angrily jerked the Ford around the sharp lefthand curve. Gravel splattered up under the car as they topped Brown's Ridge and headed downhill, toward the Ohio River and a new life.

††††††

Sam lunged against the rope, barked after the departing car, finally tired and lay curled close to the fence. Whimpering softly, he waited for Jimmy.

At sundown Homer Cox hobbled to the gate, offered a platter of gravy and biscuits, and bent to pet the anxious hound. "I'll untie you in the mornin, Sam," he said tiredly. "Better keep you tied up till the boy's plumb gone."

Sam ignored the food, and kept his eyes fixed on the empty roadway.

††††††

By midnight the hound's sharp teeth had cut the rope away, and Sam was free. He vanished into the night, running easily, settling quickly into a steady pace. An hour later he topped Brown's Ridge, stopped to lap muddy water from the ditch, and to test the wind with his sensitive nose.

Then, he continued his methodical search, padding quickly down the mountainside, following his young master.

Sam, too, was going north to the promised land.